PLAYING THROUGH THE TURNAROUND

PLAYING
THROUGH

THE TURNAROUND

Mylisa Larsen

Clarion Books
An Imprint of HarperCollins Publishers

For Patti Gauch, daemon,
who taught me what it means to be a writer

PLAYING THROUGH THE TURNAROUND

JAKE

Socks

"NO," JAKE SAYS. "JUST NO."

His mom slaps the socks down next to him on the bed. "Oh, come on, Jake," she says. "It's her big day. She's getting married."

"I don't care if she's getting sworn in as president," says Jake. "That's no reason for me to look like a tool." He picks up the socks between his thumb and forefinger. They're hot pink and silky, with huge black roses on them. They look like a scarf that Mrs. De Jaager, his science teacher, would wear on Meet the Teacher night.

His mom moves a stack of sheet music and settles herself on the bed next to him with a sigh. "Wear the socks, Jake. All the ushers are wearing them."

Okay. Two things. First, this wedding is not till sometime in May. It's March right now. That Aunt Cece is already costuming her nephews' ankles does not bode well for the sanity of anyone who knows her during this whole two-month span leading up to the wedding.

Second, there are only two ushers. Jake and his cousin

Peyton. That alone is a problem. With his square jaw and mane of blond hair, Peyton looks like a six-foot-two lion with broad shoulders and really straight teeth. Standing next to him, Jake will look like a five-foot-three secretary bird, complete with hollow chest, bad hair, and twiggy ankles.

Peyton can get away with wearing hot pink socks with roses. Peyton will make them look cool. If Peyton wears them, there will be a wave of teenage guys trying to buy socks just like them on the internet by that afternoon. By the weekend, some incredibly hip band from Amsterdam that everyone but Jake knows about will be wearing hot pink, rose-infested socks. But Jake Cranch? Nope, nope, and never. Part of surviving eighth grade is knowing what you can pull off and what you can't.

Jake has a long-term plan to kiss a girl someday before he dies. The survival of this plan requires that he avoid both adorning his unathletic body parts with roses and standing next to his cousin. He flips the socks toward his trash can. They hang from the rim like some creepy tattooed tongue.

"Mom," Jake says. "There will be three bazillion people at the wedding, just like there always are when your sister gets married. I'm pretty sure they'll be too overcome by the spectacle to notice one little usher's plain black socks."

His mom puts her hands over her face. She bends over until her forehead touches her knees. Her hair hangs almost to the floor, and from that upside-down angle, he sees how much gray streaks through it. Her muffled voice floats up through her hair. "There are matching vests," she says.

Crap.

When she sits back up, she is wiping laugh tears out of her eyes, and she's still kind of snorting every once in a while. She looks at Jake and bumps his shoulder with hers. She wants him to decide that this is funny and laugh with her and wear the socks and say everything is okay. But everything is not okay, and he is not going to do it.

Finally, she stops laughing and they sit.

"Look, Jake," she says. "It's for Aunt Cece. People are going to see you for maybe fifteen minutes max. It's not that big a deal."

Here's a little news flash for you. Moms are really great at being moms and stuff like that. But they have no idea what is or isn't a big deal.

CASSIE

Why Cassie Plays the Saxophone

THIS HAPPENED TO CASSIE back in fourth grade. In music appreciation class. That class was kind of a disaster even for the kids like her who liked music. Cassie spent most of that class telling Hayden Johnson to stop kicking the back of her chair, trying not to breathe too much (the room smelled like wet boots), and learning this song that listed the names of all fifty states. Great for the social studies unit. Death to all musical sensibility.

Cassie remembers on that particular day during class, Charlie Reacher was using a guitar pick to slowly take apart his chair. He'd been doing this during every class for the past two weeks, ever since he found the pick on the floor. He used it like a little screwdriver to undo the screws in his chair whenever Ms. Tiernan wasn't looking at him. Twenty minutes in, he would have so many screws loose that he'd have to air sit to keep the chair from going down under him. The boys who sat by him thought this was the most hilarious thing ever.

To Cassie, sitting two seats down, the whole thing seemed

stupid. And really, really uncomfortable. By the end of class, Charlie's legs would be shaking from trying to not put weight on his chair for forty minutes. But for those forty minutes, the boys around him hovered in a state of barely controlled glee. Whatever. You be you, Charlie.

So that day, the guys around Charlie were trying not to laugh, while the rest of the class droned away at "Idaho, Wyoming, Colorado, and New Mexico." Same old thing.

Except then it wasn't. Because the door to the music room opened. A lady in a glittery silver shirt stuck her head in. Asked, "Ready?"

"Come on in," Ms. Tiernan said. A bunch of adults carrying instruments filed into the room, and Ms. Tiernan gave a speech. At the beginning of next year, they would all have a choice in their musical education. They could choose chorus. Or they could choose an instrument to play and join band. So listen up and these lovely people will show us different instruments so each student can think about what they might like to play.

And it was pretty cool. Okay, really cool. The lady with the silver shirt and dangly earrings took out a flute and played a song by whatever boy band was the big thing that year. Olivia and Amayah and Jenae went into a group squeal. Cassie could see them deciding to be flutists on the spot. Then a guy with a trumpet told some jokes. (What do you call a cow that plays the trumpet? A moo-sician.) He played this superfast, show-offy thing. A drummer let a kid come up and help her make that thunder sound on the timpani. There was a clarinetist. A guy with a trombone.

The last guy got up with a saxophone. He looked like a grandpa—deep wrinkles traced through his brown skin and hair all white—but a fierce grandpa. Like maybe a grandpa who was a little mad at them for something. Didn't make jokes or talk to them in that super-friendly voice that grown-ups use on kids when they want them to be on their side. Just glared until everybody shut up. Didn't need to say a thing. Cassie was impressed.

Then he played the longest and sweetest note.

It started out soft like a whisper. But richer. Then it washed out over the room like sunshine. It went on and on and on. If that happened now, Cassie would know that he was using circular breathing. But no one in that room had heard of that back then. Everyone thought he was holding his breath that long. Cassie sure did.

Eyes got wider and wider. Charlie forgot about disassembling his chair. A "No way" came from someone behind Cassie. Cassie could feel something inside her expanding, expanding, expanding, even as she wondered how on earth this grandpa could not need the world's largest breath. And just when she was sure that the guy was going to pass out dead on the music room floor, he launched into these notes that were like a beating heart—percussive, deep, rhythmic. Then he sped it up till it was more like a heart attack. Then flicked notes like pebbles being skipped across still water. After that came a part that was like the worst argument Cassie had ever had with her dad.

And then. Then he was playing a scream. Like he'd put up with something so long that he couldn't stand it one single second longer. So he went out on the porch in front of his house and screamed until the birds flew out of the trees and the streetlights shattered.

Then silence.

There's almost never silence in fourth grade. Even when a teacher threatens kids with loss of body parts or recess. Someone will jiggle their chair. Scrape their nail against the zipper of their jacket. But this time there was silence. Utter and complete. The fierce grandpa guy stood there with his eyes closed. The class sat, frozen. They may not have been breathing.

Cassie sat, maybe still in the room, maybe somewhere else in some parallel universe. Somewhere where your blood pounded in time to sound. Somewhere where something in the middle of your chest had melted and then turned to fire. She didn't even know. It was like nothing that had ever happened to her before.

And just at that moment, when she might have been tipping into something as magical as that, Charlie Reacher's chair exploded under him. He went down in a heap of legs and flying metal chair parts. Ms. Tiernan was on the intercom to the nurse. Everyone was yelling. For the class, it was all over.

But for Cassie Byzinski, it wasn't over. Charlie could have fallen through the floor into another dimension. She wouldn't have really noticed. She was running those sounds she'd heard over and over in her head. She wanted to reach out and touch the gold metal of that saxophone to see if it was cold like you'd expect metal to be. Or if it felt warm and alive, like someone's face.

Cassie plays the saxophone because there are things she needs to say that she can't find words for. And the saxophone helps her say them. And because, sometimes, Cassie needs to scream.

LILY

The Question

SOMETIMES LILY WILL SEE the question on someone's face as they pass the middle school lunch table where she and Cassie always sit. Especially if it's a new kid who's just moved in from Maine or Ohio or something. And the question is: "Why her?"

Why, of all the kids in this middle school, does Lily Messina—the quiet, round-faced, not-as-smart-as-the-smart-kids girl—get to be Cassie Byzinski's best friend? Why Lily?

Sometimes she wants to look at them like they've said it out loud and say, "It's a long story." Just to see what they'd do.

But it isn't a long story. It's a short one.

On the second day of third grade, during recess, Lily was sitting in the alcove by her classroom door next to the bin where everybody dumps their lunch boxes and jackets and hats. She was reading. Okay, not reading, because back then reading was really hard for her, even though everybody else in her class had long since caught on. She was looking at the pictures, such beautiful pictures, in a book her nonna had given her. She was

9

looking at a kingfisher exploding out of the water after a dive, every feather along his wing tips spread out in the sun and drops of water falling around him like jewels.

When a shadow slid over her. And it was Garrett. From her class last year. The kid who picked on anyone who was alone or quiet or wore a shirt he thought was stupid or had anything about them that was different.

And here she was alone at recess, far away from the two grumpy recess monitors who would be standing together next to the playing field so they could yell at the boys if they started playing tackle football instead of touch. And none of the things that the teachers say to do to make a bully stop would work. Lily had tried them. And Garrett had said, "I don't like it when you do that" and "Stop" back to her in a jeering voice, then laughed and kept doing whatever he wanted. Or blocked her from going to tell a teacher. Or, when she did manage to get to a teacher, told that teacher that Lily was lying, so the teacher on the playground just sighed and said, "Both of you stop it, okay?"

Garrett poked her with his foot. "Let me see the book. Let me see the baby book with the pictures." She curled over her book, holding it tight, hoping that somehow, this time, he'd go away. But he hawked up a big wad of spit and let it drop right in front of her, so she had to flinch to keep it from landing on her leggings.

She knew how this would go. Spit in her hair and on her shirt, on her face. On her beautiful new book.

But just as the second gob of spit was hanging from Garrett's lips, he made an *oof* sound and slammed against the wall. Lily looked up into the sun and saw . . . someone. Someone with a halo of white light around her head like the saints in the book by Nonna's bed. The someone stepped forward, and it was the new girl. The one from Pennsylvania who had just moved in, standing there with her fists up.

"Moron," said Garrett. "Knock it off."

"Make me," said the girl, hopping around on the balls of her feet, shiny brown ponytail swinging. When Garrett came toward her, she threw an air punch at him and then another. One almost to the chin so that he stepped backwards. One to the cheekbone, almost. To the nose, almost, so that he ducked, even though she hadn't touched him since the first shove.

Garrett gave a furious shout and surged forward, trying to catch her, but she was too fast for him, dancing just out of his reach and now starting to land her punches — a quick jab to the chest, a flurry of punches to the shoulder as she whirled away, and then, as he bellowed like an angry animal and came toward her, she landed one fierce, quick punch to the nose. Garrett grabbed at his face, crying, and ran around the corner.

"Come on," said the new girl, reaching out her hand to Lily.

"He's gone to tell." She hauled Lily up, and they went to sit in the corner of the playground climbing wall, which hid them from almost everyone's view. They looked at kingfishers and blue jays and tiny hummingbirds in nests the size of a walnut.

And in one of those elementary school miracles, Lily and Cassie have been best friends ever since that moment. Even though Cassie's dad moved her away from town and then moved her back three times in the years after.

Every time Cassie moves back, kids swirl around her, asking where she's been. And Cassie can be kind of armored up and sharp with them about all the questions. But Cassie will find Lily at lunch the first day, and Lily will slide over to make room for her, and Cassie will sit down like she hasn't been gone for six months or two years, like nothing has changed. And weirdly, it seems to Lily that nothing has, and she doesn't need to ask any questions at all. Lily has always been Cassie's best friend. Even though many people want to be Cassie's best friend.

Here's the other thing Lily wants to tell those kids — the ones that look at her like, "Why Lily?" She wants to tell them that maybe Cassie needs her as much as she needs Cassie.

QUAGMIRE

Teacher Shoes

THERE ARE KIDS TEACHERS LIKE. Kids who don't correct the grammar on a teacher's slides. Kids who don't melt the ceiling tiles over their workspace in the eighth-grade chemistry lab. Kids who don't reshelve library books as a political statement. Quagmire Tiarello is not one of those kids. He's fine with that.

It's something he puts quite a bit of effort into actually.

Then there are kids that other kids like. Quagmire knows he isn't one of those, either. He never has been. Julia Prentiss had told him that in second grade.

"Go away, Quentin," she'd said from the top of the slide. "You're always getting everybody in trouble." That was true. But that was the year of Mrs. Tyler, and he had declared war on Mrs. Tyler and didn't care what or who else it cost him.

There were lots of reasons for the war, but mostly it was because of what she'd said in the hall. "I'd call a parent-teacher conference on him," he'd heard her say as he came out of the bathroom one day, "but you know his mom is such a mess, she won't do a thing about it."

And then he'd seen Ms. Kalani, the young teacher from the classroom next door, wave her hands in a panicked way to let Mrs. Tyler know that Quagmire was standing right behind her. They had gone silent—Ms. Kalani with big eyes and a hand with bright pink nails covering her mouth, Mrs. Tyler with her lips straight and tight as she watched him go back into the classroom. He'd hated her all the way to his desk. All the way through spelling words written ten times each even if you knew them already. All the way through "If your name is not neatly on your paper, it shows me you don't care."

He'd gone home that day and grabbed a handful of pepperoni out of the package in the fridge and stood and looked down at his mom asleep on the couch. He'd looked at her purplish-red hair with the brown growing out in a thick stripe on top of her head. He liked when it got stripy like that, but soon she'd probably have him paint the stripe out with one of those bottles that had a comb hooked onto the end of it. He looked at the soft drapes of skin under her eyes with the little purple veins crisscrossing them. He looked at her shirt with the buttons buttoned into the wrong buttonholes, at the spit dried white in the corners of her mouth.

Was she a mess, like Mrs. Tyler said? Was that what

made her sleep so much? Was that what made the other moms not talk to her when they went to the playground in the park?

Second grade was also when he'd learned the power of not answering. How you could get in trouble for saying something to a teacher, but they didn't know what to do if you simply didn't answer them. It made them angry, but it also confused them. And they couldn't touch you.

That still worked with most teachers even now. Which he's reminded of because he can hear Ms. Morales's cheerful voice coming down the middle school staircase. Cheerful teachers are the worst. You have to have a system with the cheerful ones—sit about two-thirds of the way back in the room and one row in from the side, in that area that's easy for a teacher's eyes to skip over. Then resist showing interest. Resist struggling. Nothing draws a teacher's eye like struggle. Nothing they feel more compelled to swoop in on. So if you don't understand what's going on, keep it to yourself. If you find the subject fascinating, likewise. You can always read up on it later when no one's watching. Saves trouble.

But Ms. Morales is new this year. Insists on calling him Quentin, a name he left behind way back in fifth grade. Insists on being cheerfully oblivious about his policy of not answering any questions in class. He's trying to discourage both these habits. He keeps his head down as he comes up the staircase on his way to physical science. Eye contact is not something he wants to risk.

He sees Ms. Morales's sandals come around the corner of the stairwell, and next to them—oh, joy—is a pair of black lace-ups, shiny as a mirror. The lace-ups step abruptly sideways to block Quagmire's path.

"Mr. Tiarello. Just the young man I wanted to speak to."

Perfect. Principal Deming. Quagmire waits for what he knows is coming. Because Deming will say . . .

"Achieving your personal best today, Mr. Tiarello?"

Quagmire refuses to play this game. A week ago, Mr. Deming called a "Spirit of Connor U. Eubanks Middle School" assembly and decreed that any time he asked a student that question, the student would reply with "Personal best is what we do at Conn U!" which was just idiotic on so many levels, not the least of them being that it made the middle school sound like a prep school for swindlers.

Quagmire had actually seen Ms. Harken, who teaches English, roll her eyes when Deming announced this gem, and everyone hates it, but most kids say it back to Deming, even if they give an ironic edge to their voices, an edge that is completely lost on Deming because he has serious deficits in the humor department and doesn't understand irony.

It's bothering Quagmire that Mr. Deming is still standing in front of him. So Quagmire steps sideways and up a step.

Mr. Deming backs up a step so that he's still a step above Quag.

Quagmire goes up one more step.

Mr. Deming goes up a step.

And now Quagmire can see the whole ridiculous scene as if it's already played out—him continuing up, step after step, and Mr. Deming, refusing to admit defeat, scrambling backwards up the stairs to stay above him until they both get to the upper hallway, at which time, on level ground—SCORE!—Quagmire will be about four inches taller than Mr. Deming.

And Quag will pause just long enough to let that sink in. Then he'll walk into science like nothing happened, leaving Mr. Deming standing outside in his shiny shoes, trying to formulate some reason to punish him. *I will now suspend you for walking up the stairs and being taller than me.*

It's going to be all about the timing, this one. And oh, Quag's going to enjoy it.

Deming is making little snorting sounds like a mad bull every time he steps backwards, and the heels of his shiny shoes clack against each stair. Quag's probably going to get detention for a week over this, but it's going to be worth it. Then he sees Ms. Harken's scuffed clogs standing still in the hall above him.

Quag's getting way too good at recognizing people by their shoes.

Now the clogs are in motion. They're coming across the floor in that determined way Ms. Harken has, and her voice is saying, "Mr. Deming, thank heavens I found you. We have a situation in the English wing that needs your immediate, immediate attention." And she's got Mr. Deming by the arm and is hustling him off down the hall before anyone even realizes what's going on.

And just before they turn the corner, she looks at Quagmire. He can't tell what that look is about. It's for him. He's sure of that. But it's not a look he's seen before. What is it? Not a warning. Not wariness. Not pity. Not even appraisal. The closest he can get to what it means is "I see you."

What's that supposed to mean?

Standing there trying to figure out this weird look makes him late to physical science. And he doesn't care about being late, but he likes to choose when he's late. Not be late because he's standing in the upper hall like an idiot, trying to figure out why some teacher with frizzy gray hair and sensible shoes gave him a look. The whole thing bugs him.

It doesn't quite sink in until halfway through science that Harken also outplayed him in the matter of Deming v. Tiarello. Swooped in and distracted Deming on purpose. Stole Quag's victory. And, okay, possibly saved him from detention, too, but what's up with that? Why should she care? He doesn't even have Ms. Harken as a teacher.

Is she trying to buy points with Quag? Like that's gonna work. She's been around forever. She should know better.

JAKE

Clarinet

IT'S 7:40 IN THE MORNING, and Mac Silva's coming down the middle school hallway, using the locker doors as a hallway-long drum set. He's thumping out jazz beats, and he's in way too good a mood for this early in the day. It's a chronic problem. This is why Jake hates seeing Mac until after ten o'clock, when he's awake enough to handle this much enthusiasm.

"Tuesday, Cranch," Mac calls out. "Gonna be a good day."

Jake gurgles an answer and leans his head against the open door of his locker. If this locker were big enough, he would crawl inside and sleep until lunch. He so does not feel like doing any of this morning.

Jake spent last night navigating three separate nightmares involving pink-and-black socks. There were giant, evil gophers trying to use his sock-adorned self for a ritual in one version. Not the best for sleep.

Mac does a final syncopated beat on the locker right next to Jake's head, which rattles Jake's skull in a way that does not improve his morning, and then Mac stops short. He stares into Jake's open locker. "Cranch, you are a disgrace to all things non-entropic," he says. If Jake were awake, he might know or care what that means, but he's not, so he doesn't move from his asleep-while-standing position.

Mac pokes at the stacks of papers and tattered notebooks spilling from the locker with a bare toe. It's getting toward the end of March, which might mean spring in some parts of the world, but upstate New York has not gotten that message, and it's stinking cold this morning. But Mac is wearing his all-year uniform of flip-flops and shorts and a T-shirt with some random saying on it. Today's T-shirt says NOXIOUS WEEDS. EVERYBODY'S PROBLEM, which Jake doesn't really understand either, and this time he doesn't think it's the earliness of the hour. A lot of Mac's shirts do not get better as you wake up.

"What are you trying to *do* in here?" Mac asks, poking a bit more. "Build a compost pile?"

Jake stares down at the heap of old papers, lunch sacks, notebooks, gym clothes, books, broken pencils, note cards. It *has* kind of built up. But they're coming to the end of third marking period. That's a lot of paper under the bridge. "I prefer to think of this as a sedimentary record of my year," Jake tells him.

Nick Finlay appears three lockers to Jake's right. He thunks down that ancient trumpet case of his and grabs a book from his locker. "Did you know that there are seventeen vending-machine-related fatalities every year in the United States?" Nick asks.

"No one cares, Nick," says Quagmire, who's just slouched over to his locker on the other side of Jake.

"Feral vending machines or tame ones?" Mac wants to know, leaning himself against the wall of lockers, which give a little squeak of protest. Mac is a big guy.

"Not specified in the data," says Nick.

"You do not want to see the marks a feral vending machine makes," Mac says. *"Ugly."*

"Take the last nutty bar, and even the most docile vending machine can turn rip-out-your-jugular crazy in the blink of an eye," says Jake.

The warning bell rings, and Mac swings his backpack up onto his shoulder. "Tuesday, guys," he says. "Just keep saying that to yourselves." And he's off down the hall, sandals slapping.

Cassie and Lily come around the corner, and Mac high-fives them both as he goes by, booming out, *"Tuesday,* people. It's *Jazz Lab* day. And we got *spring concert* coming up. So bring your game today."

Okay, first, spring concert is not till the end of May. So Mac is the only person getting excited at this point. But Mac loves a concert. Second, Jake wishes he could talk to people as easy as Mac does. Even half as easy as Mac does. Just once he would like to see Lily Messina smile at him like she just smiled at Mac.

But Jake has to make it to fourth period for Tuesday to do him any good, and he has his doubts about whether he can hang on for that long. It's worth a shot. If it were Monday, fourth period would mean Health, which is an exercise in shared trauma. Basically, a semester-long list of 271 Ways You Could Die Before You're Fourteen. Not even kidding. Lyme disease to STDs, they cover it all. No matter how good Jake feels walking into health class, less than forty-two minutes later, *bam*, he's dead. Again. Drug overdose. Hantavirus. Car crash while texting and driving. If they start a unit on signs that you've become a zombie next week, Jake will not be surprised. Worst class ever.

But, today. Today is Tuesday. If he can make it that far, on Tuesdays and Thursdays at 10:13, Jake, Mac, Cassie, Lily, and Nick all have Jazz Lab. Clarinet, piano, saxophone, upright bass, trumpet.

One time, Jake's mom took him to Syracuse University to hear this jazz quartet. It was when he was probably in fourth grade, and he was okay with going but maybe not thrilled. So Jake was twisting around in his seat before it started, trying to see up into the balcony, a little bored, and people around him were looking at their phones, or rustling their programs, or whispering, maybe a little bored too. But when the musicians came in and started playing, something happened. Like suddenly every flicker of consciousness in that crowd was pinpointed on them. They were that good.

Someday, Jake wants to be that good. Someday, he wants to play his clarinet in front of a crowd and hear the breath catch in the throats of everyone in the room over the way he plays a note. And when he plays for Mr. Lewis in Jazz Lab, Jake feels like maybe that could really happen.

CASSIE

Saxophone

BEFORE THIS YEAR, BAND CLASSES were slow. A little boring. Slow, but okay because there was music. And music got Cassie through boring. Jazz Lab, she figured, would be like that. At least, that's what she thought that first day.

All right, maybe it would be a little different. The teacher, Mr. Lewis, was this legend. Old. So old that the school had to get special permission to let him keep teaching. Cassie heard Mr. Conroy talking to Ms. Kouyate about it in the hall.

Every year, Lewis came down from the high school to the middle school. Auditioned eighth-graders for Jazz Lab. Worked with the kids who made it every Tuesday and Thursday all year. Those kids, his kids, got to join the high school jazz ensemble in ninth grade. And his high school jazz ensemble cleaned up at every competition. Every one.

So Cassie was psyched when she got in. It meant something. You didn't get in if you weren't good. And then Lily got in, which was double happy territory. Mac Silva got in, of course.

Jake Cranch made it. Jake was solid. Some orange-haired kid named Nick Finlay who she didn't really know. That was it.

But it was band class. Better musicians, harder music, sure. She was happy about that. But how different could it be?

That first day, when they played together, they were playing fine. For a first run-through. Okay, maybe not the best. Stop and start. Feeling their way.

Lewis seemed nice. This wiry old guy. Out-of-control hair. Like an owl who'd just come blowing in. Conducted with only the tiniest cues—a quick flick of an index finger, raised eyebrows a measure before they came in.

So they were following along. Trying to get to know the music. Smoothing things out. And then Lewis stopped. Cut them off in the middle of a phrase. Stood, looking over their heads. Like he was seeing something besides the stained fiberboard walls of the band room. Let them sit. Mac's hands in the air over the keys. Lily's fingers still pressed down on the strings of her big bass. Jake with his lips folded around the clarinet's black mouthpiece. Nick nervously fingering the valves of his trumpet.

"Competent," Lewis said, still staring off at nothing. "Jazzy. But not jazz." He put his hands in the pockets of his baggy khakis and jangled the keys and coins there. "Instruments back in their cases, please," he said.

Cassie lowered her saxophone. Glanced at Lily. Instruments

back in their cases? Lily shrugged, her eyes with her worried "What's going on?" look. Jake acted like he thought they'd been fired.

"Hurry," said Lewis. "We don't have all day. Instruments in cases. Mac, close up that piano."

What?

Mac lowered the keyboard cover. Nick, red-faced, reached under his chair for his battered trumpet case. Cassie started to take her sax apart. Lily carried her bass back to its big case. Jake just sat, clarinet across his knees.

Maybe they *had* been fired. Would he do that? On the first day? Maybe they weren't good enough.

Then Lewis said, "So, I'm giving you new instruments." He took off his left shoe. Handed it to Nick. Nick took it but clearly only because he couldn't think how *not* to take it. "Cassie, you'll play the folding chair leaning against that wall. Lily, chalkboard. Jake, the garbage bag in the trash can. And Mac, please play your sweatshirt zipper." Mr. Lewis finally dropped his eyes back down. Looked at them. "Jazz is about rhythm and repetition and variation. It's about listening to each other and having a conversation."

Cassie looked at the folding chair in her hands. The rip in its grungy green plastic seat. Okay. How was she supposed to play a chair?

Then Mr. Lewis said, "Let's begin."

Two things about that day. First is that sometimes when things are bad with Cassie's dad, and she feels like she's so angry she might scream, there are a few things that make the mad go away. It has to be something complicated but also beautiful or it doesn't work. Something like math or photography or music. Then it's like there's no more room for the mad, because there's too much else to think about. She can just relax into the equation. The light. The notes. It's hard to get there. But Jazz Lab. Jazz Lab always does that for her. Always gets her there. Ever since that first day.

The second thing is that you haven't really lived until you've seen Mac Silva play a sweatshirt zipper.

NICK

Trumpet

NICK'S PRETTY SURE HE ONLY GOT into Jazz Lab because Mr. Lewis knew his grandad and was being nice. And because of what happened last summer. He's pretty sure.

It's not like he doesn't work hard for it. He does. Maybe harder than anyone else. But even with all that working, Nick knows he's not brilliant at it. Not like some of the other kids. Most of the other kids. He's just okay.

He's glad he got in though. Even if sometimes he gets tired of having to work longer and harder than anyone else. He gets tired of being not the best.

But things have always been that way for Nick. He's not horrible at stuff, like he's not the last kid picked in gym. He's not the last picked for group projects. But he's nowhere near the first, either. He's just medium good at stuff, even when he works hard. So he's always been one of those kids around the edges, not an outcast, but not quite in anywhere either.

Until this year.

Nick walked out of Jazz Lab that first day, and it was lunch-time. So he went through the line like usual and then parked his tray at the condiments table for a minute. The condiments table was good because you could take your time, and it looked like you were getting ketchup for your curly fries instead of scoping out the lunchroom to see what table you could sit at without someone telling you to get lost or giving you one of those looks that said the same thing.

So Nick was scanning while trying to look like he wasn't scanning, and Mac saw him and kind of half stood up from where he was sitting and gave him a "Yo, Nick. Over here." And, standing there behind the ketchup dispenser, Nick felt something jump in his chest. Something that felt like hope. For a split second, he was worried that he might cry.

When he got over to the lunch table, Mac and Jake were still talking about that wild first day in Jazz Lab, and Mac said, "Was that *crazy* or what? Was that *amazing?* You played a *shoe!*" and they all laughed and talked about it, and Jake stole two of Nick's curly fries, but in a nice way, like they were friends. Then he gave Nick one of those peanut butter cookies his mom, who works in the middle school office, bakes for teachers' birthdays, so that made it more than fair. Even Quag was in a fairly good mood that day for once. Seemed as if he liked hearing about a teacher who did things not the usual way. Even if Quag himself wasn't in Jazz Lab.

Anyway, that's how after all those years of bouncing around, Nick finally got a lunch table where he belongs. That's how.

LILY

Bass

LILY USED TO GET SCARED in Jazz Lab. At the beginning of the year.

She'd wanted so much to get in. Because Cassie was trying out, yes, but also because playing the bass was something Lily was good at, and there was so much in school that Lily wasn't good at.

For the first few weeks, Jazz Lab felt like a different world. A world where maybe there wasn't gravity or any of the other stuff she was used to. Like maybe she would lift off from her chair and start floating around the room, thunking against the ceiling tiles and having to grab the overhead sprinklers to steady herself.

That's how wide-open and out of control it felt to her at the beginning. No sheet music some days, no syllabus, no list of rules, no grading scale. Nothing. The only thing that felt safe was hugging her bass and feeling its big body thrumming through her fingers like it always had. But everything else scared her.

"We're going to listen to each other, and we're going to play" was what Mr. Lewis had said. Lily didn't know how to do that. She didn't know what he meant.

There was nowhere to hide in Jazz Lab.

It was scary.

At first.

Lily remembers a day when she was little, maybe three or something, when, sun warm on her shoulders, she spent the whole afternoon jumping off the dock behind her house. She'd run and jump, and her dad would catch her and swim her back to the dock. Then she'd run and jump again. Again. Again. It never occurred to her that he might not catch her. She wasn't scared to fling herself as far out over the shining water as she could.

Now she knows that you can't always trust that. Now she knows that people can get distracted or busy. Or maybe decide that you should learn to swim back on your own. She's not sure what happened with her dad. But she knows you have to be careful about jumping. She's not three anymore.

But Mr. Lewis's class is different. He makes it different. Safer than the rest of the world somehow while still being exciting.

Now, more than half a year into Jazz Lab, it can feel like that sunny dock some days. It can feel like she can close her eyes and fling herself out over that sea of silvery notes, arms windmilling through the air in the sheer joy of jumping. And Mac will be there to spread out a thumping rhythm to carry her, or Cassie will wind a quick melody around her before she falls, or Nick will throw out a bright line of notes from his trumpet for her to swing from.

Someone will always be there. Someone will always catch her.

MAC

Piano

MAC CAN HEAR IT as he turns into the music hall today. That's one of the sweet things about Jazz Lab. The music starts before you even get there. It comes spilling out of the room as he comes around the corner, like always, like it's too big to be held in by something as puny as a door or walls. Mr. Lewis has the door open today and something swoony and lo-fi is playing on that turntable he keeps in there, filling up the whole hall with mellow awesome.

But you never know what it might be—one day, Monk thunking down on every note around a melody, the next, Shabaka Hutchings playing some mad improvisation on whatever instrument he happened to pick up that morning. Or some crazy-chill thing that Makaya McCraven made in his sleep. Miles and Coltrane being ice-cold cool on Tuesday. Then on Thursday, Nubya Garcia heating things up with such style that Mac's heart breaks open, and he wants to run down the hall waving his arms and yelling, "I LOVE YOU, MS. GARCIA!" Old and new all together in a sweet mix.

Last week, Lewis cranked Miles Mosley going wild with the effects pedals, and everyone's heads blew up as they turned into the hall. Mac could see it. People would turn the corner, and they'd be like "WHAAAAAAT?" and then three steps later, BLAM. BLAM. BLAM. MINDS BLOWN as they stopped dead in the hall.

This morning, as Mac gets to the door, Mr. Lewis is in there having his own little dance party. The man does NOT have moves. But he's doing the Lewis shuffle there at the front of the room, and he asks, "Mr. Silva, how is your world today?" which is what he always says. And Mac's like, "AWE. SOME," and then everybody's coming in and unpacking instruments and laughing and talking to Mr. Lewis about this or that and grabbing a Milky Way out of the bowl on the desk if they want one.

Then they're playing, and any dumb thing that might have happened before this doesn't matter anymore, because it's a good day whenever it's Jazz Lab day. Mac closes his eyes and settles into the back-and-forth of the music, settles into the happiness.

They've got their spring concert coming up in May, so Lewis is working them hard today, but even that is awesome. Lewis plays drums with them on a couple of pieces because they don't have a drummer this year and he's feeling it. In fact, they're all playing good together. So about ten minutes before bell, Lewis raises his hands and says, "Enough. Let's do a request."

YEAH!

Cassie calls out, "Cold Duck Time," and everybody's all over that. About halfway through that piece, all six of them really get together and they are BURNING UP the ROOM. Mac's slamming down on his keys, and he can hear that Cassie's playing fierce and Jake's clarinet is all crazy elegance today. Lily's throbbing away on that big bass of hers, holding them all together. Even Nick is relaxed and having fun. The band is HOT. Mac is expecting the fire alarm to go off any second.

When they finish up, Mac's high-fiving Lily and chest-bumping Jake, and Cassie's got her fist raised like she just won a race or a soccer game.

Mr. Lewis is grinning. And he says, "That was really fine playing, people. That was some nice jazz."

Then Mac's like, "WHAAAT? Mr. Lewis, was that like a COMPLIMENT I heard?" Because Lewis isn't too free-wheeling with the compliments. Mac can play like the emperor of swing and bebop combined, and Lewis'll just be like, "Good, but let's make sure we're listening to each other as we go into the turnaround." And Mac will be like, "EXCUSE ME? I just played like Art freaking TATUM," and Lewis'll be "Like Art Tatum who needs to listen to his classmates as we go into the turnaround."

So when Lewis comes back with "Yes, Mac. That was a compliment you heard," Mac's got arms in the air and is dancing behind the piano. But then something weird happens.

Sitting there at the drums, Mr. Lewis starts to cry. Not like bawling or anything, but just kind of misty-eyed like Mac's dad gets when he tells that story about how he met Mac's mom in the park when they both fell into a koi pond. Everyone goes way quiet.

Then Lewis says, "I'll go one better. Here's what I'd say. I'd say that this bunch is one of the most talented groups of musicians I've ever had the honor to play with. And that I'm proud of every single one of you, both as musicians and as people. It's been a joy to work with you and to know you."

And it's weird because instead of that making Mac double-happy-dance behind the piano, it makes him go, *"Wow,"* but a quiet wow, an inside wow. Like he's afraid to look at it too close because it's too big, too important, and he wants to save it till later when he's alone and can look at it as long as he wants to without anybody watching.

Then the bell rings and Lewis kind of brushes his eyes with

his sleeve and says, "All right. Have a wonderful day, people," like he always does, and it's business as usual.

Almost. Because Mac can still feel that *"Wow"* even as they all walk down the hall together, quieter than usual, afterward. They all can.

NICK

Fiscal

NICK'S PHONE USED TO BE about checking in with his parents when he got home from school. That was it. Just "I'm home," and then his mom texting back, "Great. Do your homework, ok?" every day so that Nick sometimes thought they should just shorten it to "home" and "homework" and be done with it. Or "h" and "h." But this year, Nick got invitations to two group chats that Mac set up—one for the lunch table and one for everyone in Jazz Lab. Nick doesn't use the Jazz Lab one too much. It's usually someone wanting to borrow sheet music from someone else or a bunch of "What's the name of that tune?" kind of stuff that Mac sends out and that Nick hardly ever knows the answer to anyway. But now when Nick's phone buzzes in ninth period, he knows it will be the lunch table group chat and Mac or Jake wanting to play video games after school—sometimes at one house, sometimes at the other. Every time it happens, it seems like a strange and shining thing to Nick. But also like something that might go away as mysteriously as it came.

Today, he and Mac are going over to Jake's house. Quag isn't coming. He didn't say why not, though Nick overheard some talk in the halls about Quag having somehow remotely taken over the projector in Mr. Ruben's class, causing one of Ruben's beloved PowerPoint presentations to cycle randomly backwards and forwards through the slides. Kids said it took five slides before Ruben even realized things were way out of order—that's how much on autopilot he can be. Mr. Ruben couldn't prove it was Quag, of course. But everyone knows Quag is good with tech, and Ruben isn't the sort of teacher who necessarily needs a lot of proof before sending a kid to detention, so that's probably where Quag is today.

Nick has to admit he won't miss him. Nick hates being on Quag's team during any video game. Quag's good, way better than anyone else at every game, but he's also way too intense about it. And if you can't keep up with him, he can be mean. Jake and Mac just play for fun.

Jake and Mac are arguing back and forth, like they do, about something in a song they played in Jazz Lab today. Nick doesn't even understand what they're talking about half the time. But he's just glad that he's walking along the street with friends instead of going home to the silent emptiness of his own house. Everybody's gone so much now, with his dad working second shift at that job that doesn't pay as much as his old job did and his mom taking extra shifts at the hospital to help make up the difference. Even when his parents get home, his house is quiet. He loves his parents, he gets along with them, but it's just them and him now and the quiet of the house, and sometimes it's too quiet.

"Dude," Mac says to Jake, "isn't that your aunt?" He's pointing out a red-white-and-blue sign in the yard they're passing. Some lady with a lot of long hair and very white teeth smiles from the center of the sign, and the words FISCAL RESPONSIBILITY TODAY, STRONG SCHOOLS TOMORROW run across the bottom in bright red letters.

"Don't!" Jake is holding out a hand like a stop sign. "We are talking about the immortal Doreen Ketchens, reigning queen of the jazz clarinet, and you dare bring up local politics?"

Mac is undeterred. "What's fizical responsibility?" he asks, squinting at the sign.

"Fiscal, not physical, Mac. Sheesh, get some glasses." And they are off down the sidewalk again, laughing.

But Nick is hanging back and picking up one of the pamphlets in the pocket on the sign and shoving it in his jacket. Because he's not quite sure what "fiscal" is either, but he's remembering last year. That day when his dad came home looking so old and tired that it scared Nick a little. That day when his dad's job got cut. That day when his dad said, "Don't trust people that use big words when they mean small things,

Nick. Because even if you call it a modest reduction in near-term head count, that's just BS for people getting fired."

And when Nick looks up some of the words in the pamphlet on his phone later that night, he doesn't feel too much better about it. "Fiscal responsibility" sounds a lot like big words for getting rid of things at the school that cost money.

Nick wonders what those things are.

JAKE

Time Travel

THE THIRD MARKING PERIOD has died in a flurry of last-chance-for-extra-credit assignments and tests no one wanted to take, and today is the first day of the new marking period. Why even bother to call it something different when it's all the same classes and same teachers, so no one really cares because nothing really changes for real?

Except that this time, it does. Because when Jake gets to English class, Ms. Cepeda isn't there. Ms. Harken is, and she's saying, "New marking period, new start. I'm taking over here while Ms. Cepeda is out on maternity leave this marking period, so choose a new seat. Let's mix it up a little."

And the seat next to Lily Messina is empty.

Jake feels his whole self go instantly sweaty. He has been trying to find an excuse to talk to Lily since fifth grade. When they both got into Jazz Lab last September, he thought this would be the year. But Lily stands over on the other side of the room near Mac's piano, and Cassie and Nick both sit between Jake and Lily, and every time he opens his mouth to talk to her, some sort of weird temporary brain dysfunction kicks in, and he suddenly has zero access to language. So he never gets to talk to Lily at all.

And now there's an empty chair, and all he has to do is slide into that chair and nonchalantly say, "Hi." And then maybe she will say hi back, and then he could say something casual but brilliant about the Don Byron piece that Mr. Lewis started them on last week. She'll smile and ask if the clarinet part is hard, and he'll roll his eyes like he's saying, "Extremely, but I got this."

But not in a braggy way.

Unfortunately, while Jake's fantasizing about this, he's also still sweating in a pretty serious way. Like a way that would get him admitted to Southton General if he wandered, dripping, past the emergency room doors. And he starts to freak out about what if Lily turns around and sees him standing here, staring, and wonders why his shirt looks like he just fell into a swimming pool. When she moves her head like maybe she *is* going to turn around, Jake panics and ducks into a desk behind Sam Armitage, who is big enough to act as a completely effective screen for a small taco truck. Then Oren Powless slides into the desk beside Lily, and it's over.

Over. Because once people stake out desks on the first day of class, nobody moves. It's like an unwritten rule. And even though Ms. Harken reset the clock for one brilliant second, Jake blew it. And the sad thing is that Sam's shoulders are so wide that Jake has to lean way to the side to even see part of Lily's left shoulder and one strand of her black hair. So he's probably going to get whatever the neck equivalent of scoliosis is by the end of the semester. Or get kicked out of school because Ms. Harken thinks he's cheating off Quag's paper, which, okay, would not be the paper anybody would choose to cheat off because half the time it's blank and the other half it has answers like *Because Miss Havisham was a doofus.* But Harken has already given Jake a "What the heck, kid?" look twice this hour, so she clearly thinks he's cheating or is deranged or has serious balance problems that are causing him to lurch sideways out of his chair or something. The whole thing's a disaster.

This is why science needs to get serious about the technology needed for time travel. Do-overs. Jake is going to die without ever having said one word to Lily Messina.

LILY

Report Cards

WHAT LILY HATES MOST about report cards are the seconds right after her dad unfolds the paper. How he smooths the page out on his desk with his blunt fingers and lets his eyes run slowly down the column of grades. It's like he's pausing to adjust himself again to the idea of a daughter who does not get As. He got As. Lily's mom got As. Lily's sister, Lauren, gets As. But now there is this other daughter. Who does not.

She knows what will happen. He'll skim down the disappointing list. He'll pick some class where she missed the next-highest grade by one or two points. He'll say, "What happened in science?"

Lily knows what he thinks. That if she'd tried a little harder on this project, or studied more for that test, she would have gotten those two magic points. That if she'd made more of those flash cards on that app he sent to her, the C on the report card would have magically become a B– that by next semester would be an A. He doesn't really believe that someone can work as hard as she can and get a 78.

"What happened in science?" he says.

She can say, "Sorry," or she can try to explain, or she can say nothing. She knows by now that there's not an answer that will make him happy.

What she wants to say is "The C is a miracle, Dad. Take the C."

If Mr. Lewis believed in grades, Lily thinks she might get an A in Jazz Lab. But Mr. Lewis says, "A grade is a pretty imperfect way of knowing how we're doing. How the music sounds tells us how we're doing. How we feel about each other tells us how we're doing." So Jazz Lab is pass/fail. And a pass, even if it's a pass that means she's learning more than she's ever learned in any other class she's ever had, isn't anything her dad wants to talk about.

CASSIE

High-Level Negotiations

CASSIE'S DAD COMES INTO THE KITCHEN, where she's doing her homework. Does that thing where he's trying to figure out whether Cassie's in a good mood without asking whether she's in a good mood. Rattles around in the cupboards. Then the fridge. Asks if she wants an Oreo.

She does. But if she takes one, it will read to him as a signal of goodwill, and she's not sure she wants to do that. Not sure she wants to let him in today. But she really does want an Oreo. She risks it. "Sure," she says.

"Milk?" he asks. Gets down one of the good, fancy glasses. So he's in serious negotiations mode.

She knows what this is about. The Event.

A.k.a. the wedding.

Well, she is not discussing the Event. It's not her event. No one asked her opinion of the Event. Or whether she wanted to go to the Event. Or even if she wanted the Event to happen at all. The Event sucks. The Event has the potential to ruin her life again. So, sorry. Five Oreos and milk in a cut-crystal glass are not going to do it.

"Celia had a great idea today," he says.

Blurrrgh. See? She knew it.

Celia. Dad's latest girlfriend. Planner of the Event. Not sure how Celia managed to talk her dad into an actual wedding. Cassie's been waiting for the whole thing to break apart. Doesn't look like it's going to. This worries Cassie. A lot.

Cassie doesn't remember her mom. At all. Super weird in a way. Cassie was the only one in the car with her when they crashed. But Cassie has zero memories. Not of the crash. Not of her mom. None. She was too little. But Celia would not be the person Cassie would pick to take over the mom spot. Even the stepmom spot.

Too bad no one asked Cassie.

Also, Cassie does not take this "great idea" thing too seriously. Celia's latest great idea had something to do with dressing everyone in the wedding in matching flapper dresses with little feathered and sequined headpieces. Yeah. Foot-long fringe plus dead birds equals not a great idea.

"No," Cassie says.

Her dad's face goes dark. He sets the jug of milk down with a thump. "You didn't even hear the idea, Cassie."

Cassie has a great idea. How about they talk about the things about the Event that she wants to talk about? Like how is this time going to be different from when he was with Miranda? Or Sheila? Is Cassie going to have to hear them yelling through the walls? Is she going to have to suddenly move? Like when she was four and she was coming home with Aunt Becca from swim lessons at the Y and then, surprise, everything Cassie owned was in the truck. And her Aunt Becca — the person Cassie's always felt was the closest thing she had to a mom — was banging on her dad's pickup window and crying and yelling at him as they backed out of the driveway and Cassie and her dad were headed to California to live with someone named Neive. Remember Neive? Blond, tall, perfect deltoids. Thought of Cassie as a cute prop to dress. Like a purse dog you didn't need a purse for.

Until Neive got bored of her. Yeah. If there had been an SPCA that took kids, Neive would have dropped Cassie off there one day while her dad was at work. Question: Would her dad have come down and gotten her back out? Let's talk about that.

Look. Celia is Neive is Sheila is Miranda. Her dad has a type. Too bad, so sad, but they're not people Cassie is interested in. Been there. Done. The only twist is that he's actually doing the whole thing up with the marriage bow this time. That's new. Don't even know what he's thinking there.

But Cassie's pretty sure nothing about this is a great idea.

Pretty sure he doesn't want her to tell him that again. He took it so well when she said it out loud last month. "No," Cassie says, and sweeps her books into her arms. Goes and locks herself in her room.

Negotiations over.

LILY

Coming Home

LILY'S FAVORITE THING IS COMING HOME. She loves getting out of the madness of the bus and walking down the lane with the light through the locust trees flickering across her face like the softest kisses. She loves walking toward the wings of the porch that spread out like arms welcoming her back.

She loves her mom's kiss on the top of her hair and her "How'd it go?" The sunshine slanting across the kitchen table. Her mom's hand as she slides a saucer toward her through that streak of light.

What Lily likes is when everybody in the family is home, and they've had a good dinner, and they aren't going anywhere at all that night. Nonna will say, "Let's just sit for a while." So they do. Dad gives Lily a book he picked up for her, and it's about lizards that run so fast they can stay on top of water, or bears that live only in a certain rain forest in Canada, and both books are full of pictures, and neither book has anything to do with school. Lauren is lying on the carpet, talking to Mom.

Nonna says something smart-mouthed to Dad that nobody else could get away with, but he laughs because it's Nonna. And then everybody laughs.

That's what Lily likes. Being home. Where no one will call on her even though her hand wasn't up. Where no one will make her work a problem on the whiteboard in front of all those eyes. Being safe. Knowing what will happen.

JAKE

Birdcages and Budget Cuts

WHEN JAKE GETS HOME after school on Wednesday, there are six enormous hot-pink birdcages with shipping tags sitting on the front porch. This has got to be something for Aunt Cece's wedding. Weird stuff has been showing up here for weeks, and if flamingos to match the cages show up tomorrow, Jake will not be surprised. Last wedding, Aunt Cece rented six of those giant poodles with ridiculous floofy haircuts so each of the bridesmaids could walk down the aisle with a poodle on one side and a groomsman on the other. Yeah. Did not know you could rent poodles, but apparently you can.

But now, besides all of Aunt Cece's crap making Jake's front porch look like a life-size Barbie aisle in Target, there is also another of those big signs in his front yard with his Aunt Terri's face smiling out from the center of it.

Great.

Jake stands and stares at the sign leering across the grass.

Apparently, it's school board reelection season again. Which is just fabulous because that means that every Saturday they aren't prepping for Aunt Cece's wedding, they'll be working on Aunt Terri's political campaign.

It also means Jake got a text from Nick last week wondering if Aunt Terri is planning on getting rid of stuff at school. And that question has been worrying Jake for days. Because how should Jake know what Aunt Terri is planning on? Like Aunt Terri bothers to share these things with him. Truth is though, she could be planning anything. Aunt Terri has ambitions. Today, Southton Falls School Board, tomorrow, archmage of the evil galactic empire in charge of clamping down on cost overruns on space cruisers.

Last time Aunt Terri got all vigilant about the school budget was when Jake was in fifth grade, and suddenly there were no field trips allowed that year, which meant Jake's class was the first set of kids since the dawn of Southton Falls time who were cheated out of the daylong ropes course thing that every other fifth-grade class before them got to go on. Jake's still mad about that.

Jake's heading up to his bedroom to begin his daily dose of confusion over the mixing of the alphabetical and numerical systems (a.k.a. algebra) when Aunt Terri's big white SUV pulls into his driveway. Great. He is not in the mood to deal with Aunt Terri right now.

But, of course, she rings the doorbell. Jake hesitates but figures if he doesn't go answer it, she will call and complain to his mom, and then his mom will text him, and he'll end up having to deal with whatever Aunt Terri wants anyway, so he just goes down. When he opens the door, and Peyton is there too, lifting the tailgate of the Suburban, Jake regrets his decision.

"Jake, honey," Aunt Terri sings out, brushing back her long hair. "Your mom said you were home. Come help unload some campaign signs from the car." She gives him a big smile, like unloading campaign signs is what every teenage boy sits around secretly longing to do and she has just made all his dreams come true.

This is what makes Jake crazy. Does she ask if he's busy? (He is.) Does she ask if there is space for her campaign signs in their laundry room? Which is apparently where these are going to be stashed, since Peyton has just leaned an armload of them against the dryer in a way that will make it impossible for Jake to get his underwear out of there. (There is not.) Does she say, "Jake, I've always believed that you adore carrying these delightfully patriotic signs with sharp wires attached that could open you up from knee to ankle, but I just want to check in with you to make sure that assumption is accurate"? ("Wildly inaccurate" does not even begin to express the level of error here.)

But when Jake pauses, hand on the doorknob, he sees Aunt Terri's smile go a little cold in the eyes. "Let me get my shoes," he says. Because he knows that behind that smile lurks danger. Aunt Terri has retractable fangs. And they become visible if you don't respond to the "Won't this be fun?" ploy. In his head, Jake refers to Aunt Terri as Aunt Scary.

Half a million campaign signs later, Jake's mom shows up to nix the brilliant pile-everything-in-front-of-the-appliances plan, so Jake and Peyton have to move all the signs to behind the kitchen table (because no one here needs to eat, either), and Jake is just about done with this whole family togetherness thing. Especially when Aunt Terri and his mom start talking about Aunt Cece and wedding plans, which Jake was totally sick of two weddings ago.

As soon as they're looking at some email from Aunt Cece with pictures of dresses, Jake retreats to his bedroom and inserts earbuds so he can't possibly hear if his mom calls him downstairs. He starts on the math soup thing. And although logarithms are kind of twisty-turny, they are not entirely stupid, and Anat Cohen playing in his ears is never stupid, so he's reasonably happy for about three and a half minutes, until Peyton sticks his head around the doorjamb.

Peyton shambles over and drops into Jake's desk chair. It rolls across the floor, probably reacting to the surprise of an extra foot and an extra fifty pounds more than it's used to.

"Hey," says Peyton, flicking Jake a cool, "I practiced this in the mirror" one-fingered wave.

"Hey," Jake says, not bothering to remove the earbuds, because even though he and Peyton are cousins and in the same grade, they have now probably exhausted what they have to say to each other for the year. Peyton belongs to the Sports Demigods caste, and Jake belongs to the Band Geeks caste, and these groups do not converse. When Jake and Peyton pass in the hall at school, they pretend they don't see each other. Geek mortals are invisible to demigods. It's some sort of rule. But even without the rule, Jake's pretty sure they would not find much to discuss.

Peyton demonstrates the truth of this by tipping his head toward one of the jazz posters on Jake's wall and asking, "Who's the dude with the flute?"

Clarinets confuse people. Jake does not know why. If you say, "Name a clarinetist," it's almost a given that the person will repeat, "A clarinetist?" like they're stalling, like they need a minute to think. Because they do. Sometimes after mumbling for a bit, older people will snap their fingers and say, "Oh! Benny Goodman!" like they're really proud of themselves, and Benny is a good one, but if you say, "What's your favorite Goodman tune?" then the whole stall pattern starts again — "Tune?" — and this time they won't pull out of the stall.

So Jake doesn't even want to get into this with Peyton, but he can't help saying, "Jimmy Hamilton, one of the greatest clarinet players ever," in a way that implies that everyone but his cousin, duh, obviously knows this.

"Oh," Peyton says, and settles back in the chair again.

Jake stares at his math homework, making it clear, he hopes, that this little attempt at cousinly chitchat should be over. His phone buzzes. It's just some spam text, but it reminds him about Nick asking about the school board. Maybe Peyton knows something about that.

"Hey. Has your mom said anything about school budget cuts coming up or anything?"

Peyton shrugs. "I dunno."

Helpful kid.

"It's important," Jake tells him. "A friend was asking about it."

Peyton leans back in the chair and drums his fingers on the armrests. "Look, she talks about that budget stuff all the time. *All* the time. I kind of don't listen anymore."

"Well, think about it," Jake says. "Did she mention anything specific?"

Peyton sighs. "They've got some meeting about the budget coming up. Like maybe they were going to try to figure out which things they could cut that wouldn't make too many people mad. Stuff that"—and here Peyton does air quotes—"only benefits a small number of students."

Jake stares across the room at his tall, blond cousin. It's like Jake can hear the words "only benefits a small number of students" echo and re-echo across the room. It's like an industrial-grade, trillion-watt lightbulb has just gone off in Jake's head, and he can see the yard sign burned into his retinas: FISCAL RESPONSIBILITY TODAY.

That's adultspeak for "We're not paying for this." The school board is looking for places to save money, and the thing that Jake loves most in the whole world "only benefits a small number of students." Are they going to get rid of Jazz Lab?

Now Jake's furious. Every time it looks like he's going to get what he wants, some adults swoop in and ruin it. Jake waited three years to try out for Jazz Lab and now, when he's in, Aunt Terri and the school board are going to kill it? Because it "only benefits a small number of students"?

Well, okay. Yes, it does. And one of the small number is Jake. That's kind of the point of an audition-only group. You have to earn your way in.

Jake turns toward his cousin. "How would you like it if the school board decided to do away with the soccer team?" Which is kind of an audition-only group too, but Jake's pretty sure no one is talking about cutting that. Not a chance.

Peyton spins himself around in the desk chair and starts poking in Jake's pencil jar. He takes out a Preservation Hall Jazz Band pencil and flips it end over end and catches it. "If you want to know the truth, I'd be glad if they did that," he says.

"What?"

"Cancelled soccer," Peyton says. "I'd be glad."

Now Jake's totally confused. Mr. Soccer? What the heck?

Peyton gives him a quick, sideways look. "Then I wouldn't have to make varsity next year."

"Don't you want to make varsity next year?"

Peyton slumps in the chair and stares up at the ceiling. "I don't know. Soccer used to be fun. But now it's all I do. Like my mom signed me up for all these camps over the summer, and now I work with a coach every single weekend. Every day it's like, 'Have you worked on foot skills for thirty minutes today?' or 'I don't want you out with friends until you've worked through at least two positioning drills.' It's not fun anymore. I think I'd be kind of glad if it all went away."

Jake stares at Peyton for a few more seconds until Peyton spins around in the chair and starts stabbing holes in a pad of Post-it notes. Jake goes back to his homework.

But he can't concentrate. If Aunt Terri is trying to get rid of Jazz Lab, every kid in there is going to hate Jake's guts. Cassie will glare, and Mac will act grieved, and Lily won't even look at him. Lily will loathe him before he ever gets a chance to say one single word to her.

Jake closes his algebra book. What if it's true? What if Aunt Terri's got Jazz Lab on her sacrificial victims budget list?

CASSIE

Coming Home

CASSIE THOUGHT AUNT BECCA would come home for the wedding. That would have been the only upside. But she isn't coming. Cassie's dad didn't invite her. Aunt Becca didn't even know about the wedding until Cassie told her. Then when Becca asked her dad about it, he was all, "Not a big deal, you don't have to ruin your trip to be here." Like he was doing Aunt Becca this big favor by not inviting her.

But Cassie knows that he just doesn't want her there.

What kind of brother doesn't invite his own sister to his wedding?

The kind who doesn't want to answer questions. Like "Are you sure this is a good idea after only three months?" Or "Have you thought about how this will affect Cassie?" The kind of brother who gets mad. Slams doors. Walks out if you question anything he does.

Yeah. Aunt Becca and Cassie's dad do not get along. Funny, because the whole rest of the world seems to get along great with Aunt Becca. Just try walking through town with her on a sunny day when people are out. Takes you forty minutes to go a block. Because every person you meet will call out, "Becca Byzinski!" Get a smile on their face like the best thing of the year is happening. Then Aunt Becca will stop and talk to them about their dachshund. Or their ferns. Or their second cousin Lucas. Or whatever.

Everybody in Southton Falls thinks of her as this prize citizen. The one who made it to the big time but who still loves this small upstate town, spread out like a fan on the north side of the lake.

Far as Cassie can tell, her dad is the only person Aunt Becca clashes with. They can't get along for more than three hours. Last time, Aunt Becca had been home for only about twenty minutes when she and Dad got into some major argument. Cassie never did find out what that was about.

But Aunt Becca always lets Cassie and her dad come back and live in the apartment over her garage when they need a place to stay. This is the fourth time Cassie has lived here, and this time her dad didn't even pretend that he was looking for a place of their own. Which is great as far as Cassie is concerned. This little apartment feels like home. Being near Aunt Bec feels like home.

Aunt Becca didn't call him on it. But that's about as far

as he can push her. He can't talk Becca into doing things like he can with other people. She's about the only person besides Cassie who is immune to Dad's charm.

So they don't get along.

But honestly, Cassie loves it when Aunt Becca comes home. She loves seeing the new photos from wherever her aunt has been shooting. A billion bats flying out of a cave against a gibbous moon. A kid jumping off a cliff into a river like he does not have one single worry about this wild drop coming or anything else in this whole big world. A soldier with his face and hair covered with dust and looking at you out of the clearest, greenest, saddest eyes on earth. A picture of an old grandma, hair thin and stringy and no teeth, but holding a little girl's hand and laughing like that little girl just told her the best joke she's ever heard.

That one was for a piece in *National Geographic*. The bats were in a show at the Smithsonian. Aunt Becca says it's not that big a deal. It is. She's been all over the world with her cameras. In caves, in tombs, at festivals, or just in a corner store in Jakarta, taking pictures. Pictures that make you feel like you were there too.

Also, when Aunt Becca's home, Cassie can talk to her about stuff. Tell her the things that make Cassie really mad. Aunt Becca doesn't get all worried or embarrassed. Or give her a pep talk about getting along with her dad. How these teenage years are difficult for everyone. She just says, "Uh-huh, uh-huh, I hear you," and then after a while she'll say, "Ice cream or popcorn, Winnie the Pooh?" which is her joke, because Cassie used to always say, "Both," like Pooh Bear does when Rabbit asks him if he wants honey or milk with his bread. And then they'll watch a movie together, eating the ice cream straight out of the cartons.

Tonight, Cassie gets out her phone before she goes to bed and sends Aunt Becca a text: "Miss you."

Cassie knows that Aunt Becca is probably asleep right now halfway around the world in a place called Svalbard, and Cassie hates the lag time. But Cassie also knows that when she wakes up in the morning, Aunt Becca will have texted back. She always does.

Always.

QUAGMIRE

Ms. Harken

QUAGMIRE HAS WAITED FOR WEEKS for Ms. Harken to try to cash in on getting Mr. Deming off his case. But she hasn't. Doesn't stop him in the hall to encourage him to work a little harder in school. Doesn't argue for keeping the peace. Doesn't even look at him when she passes. Nothing. Like he doesn't exist. Like the whole "Here, let me spring you from Deming" thing never happened.

Like she doesn't know who Quagmire is. Or care.

Even when Harken takes over his English class at the beginning of the new marking period, she avoids the usual fracas about his name by just reading out "Quagmire Tiarello" when she calls roll, like it's any other name. Doesn't try to force the Quentin. Doesn't finesse it by calling all the students in the class by their last names. Doesn't try to get cute by calling him Q. Just "Quagmire Tiarello." And when he doesn't answer, she puts a check by his name like she's done with every student who answered, "Here."

Then she leaves him strictly alone. For a week. Then a week and a half. Doesn't ask him questions. Doesn't call on him in class to see if she can trick him into answering. Actually skips him when they take turns reading aloud from *Romeo and Juliet*. (Which, by the way, Quag has already read and decided that both principal characters were pretty dim bulbs who probably deserved each other. Romeo and Juliet: co-winners of the Darwin Award in 1597.)

Class after class after class, this goes on. Like he's not there. By the middle of April, the whole thing's bugging him. He thinks about starting some sort of trouble in her class. Or just raising his hand to answer a question. But what if that's what she's waiting for? If it is, then he loses. No. He can outwait her.

When he comes in over fifteen minutes late one day (Coach Brody felt the need to start off his Thursday afternoon by yelling at someone, and Quag was the someone), he wonders if she'll finally say something, because Brody didn't give him a hall pass, and Quag certainly did not feel the need to ask for one. But when he opens the door to her class, none of the other kids are there. Just Ms. Harken standing over her desk, scribbling something on a Post-it note. "Oh, good," she says. "We're in the computer lab today. I was leaving you a note."

So they walk down to the computer lab together. And she

doesn't try to make conversation or ask where he was or try to ferret out what his interests are or inquire after his psychological well-being or anything. The computer lab is clear on the other side of the quad and up the back staircase, and all you can hear is the clunking of Ms. Harken's clogs and the shushing of Quag's sneakers, and to tell you the truth, this walk is feeling way longer than it usually does with only the *clunk shush, clunk shush* of the shoes going on and on and on. But she seems completely fine with the silence, and he's not going to ask her how her day is going. Nope.

When they get to the intersection of the hallways where they should turn right, she turns left, and for some reason (probably the hypnotic effect of the *clunk shush, clunk shush*), Quagmire turns with her. "Just have a quick errand I need to do," she says, and opens up one of those hallway doors without windows that usually lead to a closet. It is a closet, but a big one, and, super weirdly, there is a man with headphones on sitting in there in an office chair. The walls on either side of the room are crowded with racks of electronic equipment. There's a poster of some guy with some seriously wild hair heading a soccer ball hanging over a scuffed table against the back wall. A huge set of speakers is stacked in the corner, and there's a pegboard with maybe a hundred different cables hanging from it. The guy with the headphones is bouncing around in his chair, clearly listening to some tunes and not even aware that his weird inner sanctum in a closet has been breached.

When Ms. Harken touches him on the shoulder, Headphones Guy kind of turns around and nods at her but keeps drumming the arms of his chair for a few seconds and closes his eyes like he's listening to something that cannot be interrupted. Which, apparently, Ms. Harken is okay with, because she leans against the doorframe until the guy finally closes out whatever song he's listening to, sighs contentedly, takes off the headphones, and says, "Ms. Harken, how may I assist?"

"Still looking for kids for tech crew?"

"Got a couple spots."

"Well, this is the young man I was telling you about. He's intelligent. He's tech-savvy. I think he'd be able to handle anything you can throw at him."

Really? Quag is a little disappointed in Ms. Harken. He's been worried about being strategically outplayed, and all she's got is the old let's-get-him-involved-in-an-after-school-activity-where-he-can-feel-a-part-of-something-larger-than-himself-and-maybe-he-won't-be-such-a-pain-in-the-butt-at-school ploy?

No way. Not happening.

"Great," says the dude in the headphones, and he spins around to grab a slip of blue paper off his desk. "Come up during your study hall, and I'll walk you around the stage and show you what you'll be running. I need somebody good with tech up in the box."

Quag takes the slip of paper the guy is waving at him, even though he is not planning on showing up during study hall. Not happening. Not happening. Not happening. It's a hall pass, but it's been modified with a GET OUT OF JAIL FREE stamp featuring the Monopoly guy in his striped prison pajamas.

"All right, let's get to the computer lab," says Ms. Harken, as if Quag has said yes, as if everything is all set now. It isn't, but let her find that out later. She turns to head out of the closet when Quag hears the sharp *clack, clack, clack* of what can only be a pair of shiny-as-mirrors lace-ups.

"What's going on here?" demands Mr. Deming, stopping outside the door of the closet/office and looking back and forth from the headphones guy to Ms. Harken to Quag, as if he's caught them in the middle of a drug deal.

"New member of tech team for the spring musical," says the young guy with the headphones, nodding toward Quagmire. Out of the corner of his eye, Quag sees Ms. Harken briefly close her eyes and flare her nostrils. She wishes Headphones Guy hadn't said that. Not to Mr. Deming.

"We were just heading down to work on some research for English class at the computer lab," Ms. Harken says. "Come along, Mr. Tiarello." And she starts out the door.

But Deming is not going to let this slide. "Ms. Harken, Mr. Saavedra, may I remind you that responsibilities like tech crew are reserved for highly motivated learners who show a sense of respect for the spirit of Connor U. Eubanks Middle School and demonstrate partnership and community?" The fluorescent lights in the hall reflect off his gleaming shoes and his perfectly parted black hair. He puts his hands in the pockets of his blue wool suit pants with the knife-sharp creases, and Quagmire wants to reach out and twist his burgundy tie around and around until that smug face turns red and then blue and he drops to the floor. And then Quag will walk out of this stinking school and tell his mom to get everything in the car and they'll start driving. And wherever they end up, at least it won't be here.

But he hears himself say, "Fine with me. It was just for community service anyway. I got in trouble in gym, and Coach said I had to stay after this week and scrub down the floor of the stage to make up for walking the mile run."

You want to go, Deming? Let's go. Let's see who wins this round.

"Ah," says Mr. Deming, jingling the keys in his pockets. "Ah. Community service. Well then. Just see that he's supervised at all times, Mr. Saavedra." And he continues his *clack, clack, clack*ing down the hall.

Ms. Harken and Quag take off for the computer lab as soon as the clacks go around the corner. The lockers stretch out down the hall on either side of them in banks of vivid blue. They travel under row after row of fluorescent lights. They still have not said one word to each other, but Quag wonders if it's just his imagination that the *clunk shush* of their shoe duet sounds oddly jubilant.

NICK

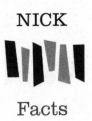

Facts

NICK CAN'T STOP THINKING about that sign they saw. FISCAL RESPONSIBILITY, it said. He even looked both words up again — this time in the old blue dictionary from the bookcase in the hallway.

"Fiscal" just means "having to do with money," and "responsibility" means "being trustworthy." Being trustworthy with money's got to be a good thing, right?

So how come every time Nick walks around a corner and sees those two words together on another campaign sign stuck in somebody's yard, he gets a little stomachache?

LILY

Speak Up

PEOPLE ARE ALWAYS TELLING LILY to speak up. "Speak up, Lily," her dad says when he asks her about her day. Teachers say it when they've asked her a question. When she came down to the counselor's office today to fill out her class schedule for high school next year, the counselor said, "Could you speak up, honey? I'm having a hard time hearing you," and then the counselor rattled off which classes she thought Lily should take and filled them in herself without ever stopping to see if Lily had anything to say or not.

So now Lily's sitting in that hard orange chair across the desk, with the counselor talking about the high school bell schedule, and she thinks about when she was little and how she used to run through the halls of the house with her sister on those endless sunny mornings you get when you're a kid, yelling just to hear themselves yell. Filling up the space with themselves. Not even imagining that someone might not want to hear them.

But after a while, Lily noticed: They want her to speak up

when she agrees with them. When she wants to do exactly what they want her to do.

Not when she's saying no.

They want her to speak up when she has the right answer.

Not when she's saying, "I don't know."

Not when she's saying, "I feel stupid."

Not when she's saying, "I hate reading."

Not when she's saying, for the fifth time, "I still don't understand."

They say they want her to speak up, but she notices how relieved they are when she nods and pretends she's got it. Because now she fits back into the world they wanted.

It's so much easier to be quiet now that she's noticed that no one really wants to hear what she's saying anyway.

QUAGMIRE

Hall Pass

WHEN THEY GET TO THE COMPUTER LAB, Ms. Harken logs Quagmire on to some website about American poets and gives him a list of possible names for research. Quag slumps into the chair in front of the screen and clicks around without really reading anything until Ms. Harken finally moves to another part of the room.

Then he googles "soccer players with crazy hair," which turns up the fact that the soccer player on the poster in Headphones Guy's closet is Carlos Valderrama, who played for Colombia way back before Quagmire was even born. It also turns up a 25 Worst Hairstyles in Soccer History site, which is a pretty epic way to spend the rest of the period.

Quagmire has no intention of going anywhere except study hall ninth hour. But he feels the hall pass folded up in his pocket as he scrolls through soccer players from the eighties and keeps an eye on where Ms. Harken is in the room. He feels it there as he walks through the crowded hall after English and down the stairs and back into the main wing.

The next class doesn't present much of an opportunity for amusement, so by study hall, Quag is dying of boredom. Possibly literally. He can feel brain cell after brain cell shrieking and then going dark.

He pushes through the halls, where the usual overwrought tide of humanity is having the usual drama, and gets to his usual study hall, where Ms. Pham throws him her usual "No messing around" look as he comes in. He slides into his usual desk on the back left side and stares out over the rows of desks and the usual upbeat posters above the whiteboard and the usual bank of windows that face out on a blank brick wall.

Why bother with windows if you're gonna look at a wall?

The blower clicks on, which is always bad news in this class, because it means that it's about to get way too hot or way too cold. The corner of the TODAY IS A GREAT DAY FOR A GREAT DAY poster rattles maddeningly, as it always does when the air from the ceiling vent hits it.

And suddenly Quag can't stand it anymore. Any of it. He cannot sit here for another forty-two minutes watching Alex Grant pretend not to flex his various muscle groups in order to impress Kiarra Williams sitting behind him. Or listen to Zivah whisper the latest to Eliana about her on-again, off-again relationship with Javon Green. Or hear the squeaking of Raimy Thompson's chair as Raimy bounces his leg up and down, up and down, up and down.

He can't.

Maybe he can start a fight—either with the teacher or some kid. Or maybe . . . He pulls the hall pass out of his jeans pocket and smooths it on his desk. The Monopoly guy looks up at him, and he knows that the guy's smiling under that big mustache. Quag picks up his backpack, goes to the front, and flashes the pass at Ms. Pham.

"Sign out," she says, and waves him toward the door.

And just like that, he's free. Or as free as he can be in hostile territory, where any teacher in any hall could look up and call him out on where he's supposed to be. The trick is to find somewhere no one will find you. Or to keep moving but not repeat halls.

Then, just as Quag is heading toward the math wing, Headphones Guy, minus his headphones but with a bunch of cables looped over his shoulder, comes sweeping around the corner. "Oh, good," he says, readjusting the cables, "glad I caught you. I couldn't remember where I told you to meet me, so I came down to tell you we'll be on the stage. Mind helping me with some of this cable? We've gotta hang overhead mikes for the choir concert tonight."

Great.

There goes freedom.

QUAGMIRE

Stage Presence

HEADPHONES GUY'S PHONE BUZZES. He's standing on a ladder as Quagmire does the not-any-less-boring-than-study-hall job of handing up loops of speaker wire so that Headphones Guy can hang them above the stage. "Uh-oh," Headphones Guy says as he looks at the screen. "Trouble in the computer lab." He takes a couple of loops of speaker wire from around his neck and, climbing down, hangs them over one of the ladder's steps.

"This might take a while." He digs in his pocket. "Here," he says, and then a lanyard, prickly with keys, is sailing through the air toward Quag.

It surprises him. First, because it's such a boatload of keys. It comes through the air with weight and substance, the keys a splayed, jagged mass of metal that will put some serious divots in the floor of the stage if he doesn't catch them. And also because he is the sort of kid that teachers don't just hand their keys over to.

And for some reason, that surprise makes Quag stretch his

hand out into the dusty beam of light coming through a rip in one of the black auditorium curtains and catch the bristling mass of keys. The lanyard wraps itself around his wrist.

Headphones Guy is already striding off down the aisle through the auditorium, tapping at the screen of his phone. "The key with green tape is the door to the balcony. Orange is the sound booth," he calls back over his shoulder, gesturing vaguely upward. "Go up and mess around while I go figure out how one sixth-grade global class has managed to simultaneously crash twenty-three computers." There is the clunk of Headphones Guy hitting the crash bar on the auditorium door, and then he's gone. Quag watches the door slowly swing back and seal itself with a gentle *whoosh*, closing him into the quiet of the empty auditorium.

Why would he want to go up on the balcony?

He finds a metal door marked BALCO (apparently, they couldn't afford an *N* or a *Y*) at the back of the auditorium and inserts a key whose head is wrapped in lime-green papery tape printed with tiny iguanas. The key slides into the heavy door-knob with a satisfying click, and Quag hears a metallic pop as he turns it. The door swings inward.

Stairs rise straight up from the door. Quag feels around for a light switch. Doesn't seem to be one. Which seems a little wrong, because some genius has painted the walls, steps, and ceiling black, so the whole staircase sort of disappears into the gloom. Quag clicks on his phone's flashlight and starts up.

The steps are narrow and steep and apparently hollow, because they boom as he makes his way around a tight curve. At the top of the stairs is a tiny triangular landing hardly big enough to stand on and another metal door.

Quag finds the orange-wrapped key and slips it into the lock. This door opens outward (Seriously? What idiot was in charge of construction here?), so Quag has to move off the landing and down a stair to avoid being swept off by the door.

Inside, the light from his phone shows a whiteboard on wheels—with the pathetically cheerful slogan *TEAM: Together Everyone Achieves More* scrawled across it in purple marker—half blocking the doorway. Quag slides around the door, pulls himself up the last step, pushes past the whiteboard, and stops.

Whoa!

Glass wraps around three sides of a room that juts down from the ceiling of the auditorium. He is floating in this glass room, floating above everything—above the quiet, folded seats, above the coils of wire still draped over the ladder, above a jumble of music stands piled together backstage like they've been thrown there by some music-hating giant, above banks of lights tethered to girders high over the audience's head. He can see everything from up here.

This room owns a light switch. Or rather, a slider switch. Quag slides it up, watching the ceiling cans go from a dim glow to glaring white. And in that brilliant light, he sees, resting on a long, built-in platform that stretches across the whole front of this nest-in-the-sky room, a machine. A machine with knobs and sliders and rocker switches, with dials and displays, with cords like multicolored electronic spaghetti hanging down behind it. A machine that Quagmire wants to touch.

He rubs the fingers of his hand against his palm, looking at the nameplate—QUANTUM 5000E—somehow knowing just how hard he'll have to press the switch to turn it on, how it will tilt under his fingers, not abruptly, but just settle into place, how the lights below each knob will glow a beautiful, soft green, how the grooved edges of the knobs will feel against his fingers.

He reaches out and fits his fingertips to the switch labeled POWER. He lets them rest there against the sleek, cool, black surface and then presses.

CASSIE

In the Booth

WHEN CASSIE GETS UP to the sound booth after school on Thursday, Quagmire Tiarello is already in there. Quagmire. Such a stupid name, and Cassie would refuse to play his game and call him that, except she literally does not know what his real name is. How does he get away with stuff like this? Insisting that everyone, even teachers, call him by this super-dissy name?

And how come, when everybody else on drama crew had to go through this whole interview process and mandatory training meetings, Mr. Quagmire Tiarello can just appear, three-quarters of the way through rehearsals for the spring musical, anointed by Mr. Saavedra to the high post of soundman? Which, okay, Chuckie Pearson, who was supposed to do that, went and got mono. But it's not like there aren't six or seven other, more competent people who at least know what an accent mike is that Mr. Saavedra could have pulled in to do this.

Probably Saavedra will be all, "Cassie, if you could just bring Quagmire up to speed." So she'll have to try to explain two and a half years' worth of stuff in forty-five minutes or less. Then end up having to do half his job besides her own job of running the lights. The whole thing pisses her off.

Being on crew for the spring musical is one of Cassie's things. This is how Cassie's year is supposed to go — help with the photography club's winter exhibit, then run lights for the spring musical rehearsals, then perform in the spring concert for Jazz Lab, then finish out the year running lights for the spring musical performances. That's how it should go. And Quagmire Tiarello is about the last person she wants messing up her system.

He already sits with the three boys from Jazz Lab at lunch. That kind of annoys Cassie too. Because of all her things, Jazz Lab has become her thing of things as this year has gone by. The highlight of every Tuesday and Thursday. And some days she wouldn't mind if she and Lily sat with the other Jazz Lab kids at lunch, continuing some conversation they'd started in class.

But there Quag always is, already at their lunch table. With that sly, calculating smile. And she's like, "Nope, not dealing with that" and moving on to her and Lily's usual table. She doesn't know what the Jazz Lab guys see in him. So she is not going to let him mess up the sound booth, too.

"You're sitting in my chair," she says to him. Because he is. Chuckie and she had an agreement. Cassie gets the spinny chair. Chuckie gets the cushy but somewhat derelict chair. And

Quagmire is sitting in the spinny chair. Leaving the creaky chair that leans back too far for her. She hates that chair!

He turns his head. Looks at her. He has these eyes that aren't really one color. They're gray. Or maybe green. But they have this warm gold color splashing out from the pupil. Like there's an explosion starting there. They would be really interesting eyes, almost beautiful. Except that they're kind of expression-less. Like the only thing he ever uses them for is trying to spot weakness in other people.

Then, having seen whatever it was he was trying to see, he puts his headphones on, spins back around (in her chair!), and starts fiddling with the soundboard. So apparently, this conversation is over.

Such a jerk!

NICK

More Facts

NICK READ SOMEWHERE THAT KING TUT had two trumpets buried with him. Some people say the trumpets are cursed. That every time a person plays one, a major or minor war breaks out. It would be kind of hard to tell, Nick thinks. Seems like a major or minor war breaks out about every three days. Anyway, they probably got those trumpets locked up in a safe somewhere, just in case, so a bunch of archaeologists messing around on their lunch hour don't start World War III.

There's a guy in Indonesia who built a trumpet that's like 104 feet long. But in the YouTube video, it only plays one note over and over, like HONK, HONK, HONK. Also, it's played by a compressor or something. So here's the deal: no lips, no valves, not a trumpet. Just a really large trumpet wannabe.

Dizzy Gillespie used to play these weird trumpets with the bell bent forty-five degrees up toward the ceiling. He told everybody that someone stepped on his trumpet during a party that got a little out of control and that it sounded better, so he had all his trumpets made like that afterward. A guy who wrote a book about Dizzy said Dizzy was lying, and that's not what really happened. But what really happened is more boring, so Nick thinks probably everyone will keep pretending it happened like Dizzy said it did because it's a way better story.

So the truth is that Nick didn't really choose the trumpet. What happened was that back at the beginning of fifth grade, his mom got it into her head that he should play in band instead of sing in chorus. She'd had to go to three fourth-grade chorus concerts the year before, so Nick gets why she thought this was a great idea. But that's only because she hadn't been to a fifth-grade band concert yet. Way worse. So joke's on his mom.

Anyway, she wanted him to try band. He was like, "Whatever," but then there was the problem of money, like always. Because chorus is free, but for band you need an instrument. That was when his grandad, who was living with them then, got up from his chair and went to his room. Came back with a banged-up case.

"Oh, Dad. Are you sure?" his mom said, but his grandad waved her away with some comment about his lungs being in no shape for a trumpet anymore. So that was that. They didn't even seriously consider other possibilities. Nick played trumpet.

Not gonna lie. It was ugly. Loud, squawky ugly. For years. But what were his parents supposed to say? "Kid, you suck at trumpet. Can you please stop playing it?"

They're parents. They gotta say good job, keep practicing,

all that stuff. Nick did notice that his dad had a habit of going out to his workshop the minute Nick's mom would say, "Time to practice." Parents sometimes think they're sneakier than they are.

His grandad tried to show him some stuff. But he was right. His lungs weren't really up for trumpet playing at that point.

Nick's glad he kept at it though. He is. He wasn't for a long time. But now he's glad. All his best friends are in Jazz Lab.

JAKE

At the Lunch Table

"I GOT RID OF COACH BRODY for you," says Quagmire as Jake and Mac walk up to the lunch table on Wednesday. *This should be interesting,* thinks Jake. Being friends with Quag has its definite downsides, but one of the upsides is that life is 93 percent more interesting with Quag around.

Mac hesitates halfway into lowering himself onto one of those ridiculous blue plastic discs that serve as chairs in this cafeteria. He is wearing an even more random than usual shirt—BEWARE THE VAMPIRE SQUID. "Really?" he asks.

"Would I lie to you?" says Quagmire. Mac raises his eyebrows, and Jake pauses in the middle of peeling his banana. Because Quagmire kind of prides himself on lying, and while he doesn't lie to *them* that often, when you put it right out there as a question—"Would I lie to you?"—then in Quag's case it seems way less rhetorical to Jake than it might coming from someone else.

Quag rolls his eyes. "Never mind," he says, waving his

hand like he's erasing the question. "But I did get rid of Coach Brody. Permanently."

Mac made the mistake of actually sprinting during the track unit in gym three weeks ago, and now Coach knows that Mac can move all 234 pounds of himself with both speed and grace. Coach has been relentlessly recruiting Mac for the football team ever since.

Mac is horrified by this. Jake's heard way too much about it in the past couple of weeks.

"Is he kidding?" Mac had asked them the first time Coach stopped in the locker room after gym class to clap him on the back and tell him how much they needed him next fall on the line. "I could break a finger. Aren't linebackers the guys in the middle who run into each other repeatedly? I could break all my fingers." Since Mac plays piano in Jazz Lab, and guitar, and whatever other string or rhythm instrument they need (he can play more instruments than the rest of them put together), Mac breaking a finger would be a catastrophe for them all.

Mac was still standing in the locker room, looking horrified. "Guys, I could get concussed!" They'd covered "Concussions and You" in Health last month. It's possible that Mac pays too much attention in that class. He's fainted twice during those films they show in there.

"For the glory of the team though." Quag pulled a T-shirt down over his skinny, not-going-to-be-recruited-for-the-line chest. "Go, Tigers. Besides, you know that an upstanding authority figure like Coach Brody would never jeopardize one of his own students by convincing him to participate in a sport that was dangerous."

"Tell that to the NFL players' union," Jake said, wrestling his also-not-going-to-be-recruited puny arms out of his sweatshirt. He wondered for about half a second what it would feel like to be involved in some extracurricular activity that had whole grandstands cheering for you instead of the handful of parents and grandparents they got for jazz concerts, but then moved on. Jake liked to keep his daydreams in the realm of the possible. Besides, he loved Jazz Lab.

Anyway, Coach B wasn't kidding, because he's spent the last three weeks trying to convince Mac to come to summer football camp. Mac has spent the last three weeks ducking into bathroom stalls, empty science classrooms, and once, in a pinch, the nurse's office, where he had to invent a sudden headache and nausea. (Probably psychosomatic concussion symptoms.) The whole thing is getting to be a drain on Mac's psychological resources.

"Why don't you just tell him to get lost?" Jake asked him after Mac had hauled Jake into a janitorial closet with him to avoid Brody when he was coming down the English hall.

"I tried," said Mac. "He didn't listen. Just went on and on about me being such a help to the team and living up to my potential and stuff. I don't want to hurt his feelings, but I'm hoping he'll just forget about it if he doesn't see me around." This is the trouble with Mac. He's one of those nice, cooperative kids that adults like, but he sometimes overdoes it. So if Quag's worked some lose-Brody magic, it would be a relief to everyone.

"Explain," says Jake.

Mac finally lowers himself all the way, and their table gives a little shudder. "Yeah. How'd you ditch Coach?" he says.

"Told him you were Buddhist and your family practices nonviolence. Football is organized violence. Ergo, your Buddhist self can't be a linebacker for him."

Jake snorts. This is classic Quag.

"Dude, I'm a Mormon," says Mac.

"Yeah, well, he doesn't know what that is, so Buddhist works better," says Quag. "You owe me." As if changing Mac from one religion to another is no big deal. Which to Quag, it probably isn't. But to Mac, it might be. Music and church are about the only things Mac is serious about, and he's pretty serious about both.

"If it works, I owe you," agrees Mac.

"Hey," says Nick, slapping down a lunch tray and sitting across from Jake. "Did you know that strawberries aren't actually fruit?"

"No one cares, Nick," says Quagmire.

"I care," says Mac. "Strawberries are like the best thing in fruit salad. Fruit smoothies are made of strawberries. How are strawberries not fruit?"

"They're fleshy receptacles," says Nick.

"You're a fleshy receptacle, Nick," says Quagmire.

"No, really," says Nick. "Strawberries, which technically aren't berries, either—"

Mac slams both big palms on the table, causing serious tremors through the applesauce compartment of Nick's tray. "Strawberries aren't berries? What are you saying, Nick? That my entire childhood was a lie?"

"Your entire childhood was based on strawberries?" Jake asks him.

"Pretty much."

"Shut up and listen," says Nick. "Strawberries are not fruit. They are not berries. They are categorized"—here he shoots a quelling look at Quag—"as fleshy receptacles. *But* the little seeds on the outside, which are called achenes, *are* actually fruits."

"Thank you, Nick, for yet another useless piece of information," says Quagmire, but then everyone shuts up, because Cassie Byzinski has shown up at their table. She's standing there, looking at them.

Cassie Byzinski is gorgeous. This was established irrefutably by a vote taken back at the beginning of the year when Nick was going through his polling phase before he moved on to his oversharing-of-scientific-facts phase.

But Cassie is also dangerous. Jake has serious respect for her saxophone skills, and they get along fine in Jazz Lab, but Jazz Lab is a special case where the usual rules of middle school do not apply. When not in Jazz Lab, Jake is always aware that Cassie broke Garrett Crenshaw's nose back in third grade. She gives out the vibe that your nose could be next if you're not careful. So outside of Jazz Lab, Jake stays out of Cassie's way.

Cassie has lots of complicated rules that she enforces. Rules of behavior. Things that are or are not okay to say. Intricate food rules having to do with the good of the planet. At the moment, she is probably eating only grains grown in states starting with the letter *W*. If you break her rules, she will use you for claw-sharpening practice. Jake once saw her verbally take down Alex Grant, who always deserves pretty much anything he gets, and it was the single time in his life that Jake felt sorry for Alex.

Right now, Cassie's hair is done up in some kind of bewildering style with lots of clips. It's a little disorienting. Jake's pretty sure the hair is a distraction. You should not look at the hair. If you look at the hair and your concentration slips for even a second, you will be a goner.

There's a pause at the table while they all mentally assess their overprocessed, high-fat, possibly-carcinogen-laden-if-not-toxic-to-the-whole-planet lunches. Nick has gone white and is sweating. Then Quagmire picks up a Cheeto and deliberately licks the cheese powder off it.

Quagmire is dead.

But Cassie doesn't seem to notice. "Hey," she says. "Mr. Lewis is quitting."

Silence at the table. A sudden and immense silence like they are all holding their breath. The roar of the cafeteria shears away. Jake can feel the shift of tectonic plates under his feet.

This can't be true.

Mr. Lewis wouldn't quit. Mr. Lewis is an institution. Institutions sometimes get killed in plane crashes or something, but they don't quit. They don't. She can't be right.

But Cassie. Jake looks at Cassie, and she looks at him, and instead of the fierce look he's seen on that face every day since she moved here in third grade, her face looks like a face you'd see carved in marble in those super-depressing old statues of a lady whose whole village was slaughtered by invaders. Her face looks like she's just lost something she can't live without.

Maybe Mr. Lewis *is* quitting.

MAC

Alive

MOST CLASSES, THE TEACHERS TELL everyone
what to do. Even when they pretend not to, even when they're
like, "Get creative," they give out a rubric, or something,
that—BOOM SHAKA LAKA—pulls everyone back to
doing things their way. Not Mr. Lewis.

Sometimes in Jazz Lab, they'll have certain pieces they're
working on, but lots of times they just jam. They toss a melody
or a rhythm around the room—Mac to Lily to Jake to Cassie
to Nick and back around again until, ZIP, ZAP, the notes spin
through Mac's fingers and twine through his hair and buzz
in his ears and even the half-moons on his toenails are happy.

If Mac can make it work, Lewis will let him do it. Even if
he tries something and crashes and burns and SPLATS big-time
against the wall, Lewis is just like, "Interesting experiment,
Mac." Sometimes during Jazz Lab, Mac feels like he might
live forever.

Mac met Mr. Lewis back in fifth grade. Lewis had noticed
Mac messing around on the piano before an elementary band

concert. He found Mac's mom afterward and gave her the name of a piano teacher who wasn't so much about playing exactly what was on the page. Told Mac's mom about some jam sessions up in Syracuse that Mac could drop in on.

Mac can still remember his mom double-checking the address on her phone and then taking him down the steps to some basement dive bar, muttering, "I can't believe I'm doing this" as she held his hand for a minute. Held his HAND! In FIFTH GRADE! It was a Saturday morning, so nobody was there except the jazz people. The place wasn't even open. Still. It was kind of not the usual Silva family outing.

But then she met all the old guys who jammed together there, and she met Ms. Chantelle, who sang with them, and it's kind of hard not to like all those people, so after that first day of his mom sitting in the corner pretending to read a book but really watching everything everybody did and said, she was okay with it. Brought him every Saturday for a year and a half until that place got shut down by the city.

Because she saw how happy it made Mac to hang out with people who got music like Mac got music. Saw how they let him play like he was one of them, even though he was just a kid. Saw how the music just filled him up, SHLOOP, and he could live off those Saturday mornings for days, all those good sounds bouncing around in his head and linking up with other sounds and coming out all new.

Mac thinks sometimes about what if Mr. Lewis had never said anything to his mom. What if Mac had kept going to that piano teacher who was all about metronomes and exercises? To a place where it felt like music got locked so tight into a tiny, strict box that it might curl up and die? Mac kinda thinks Mr. Lewis rescued music for him.

And then this year there was Jazz Lab. And next year there would be Jazz Ensemble. And the year after that and that. And then who knows what.

So when Cassie says Mr. Lewis is quitting, it feels like she's saying the sun is quitting. And a big dark sheet of nothing is, WHOOSH, sliding across the face of the earth.

CASSIE

Do Something

LILY COMES OVER from their usual lunch table. Joins Cassie at the boys' lunch table.

"Why?" asks Mac. "Why would Lewis quit?"

Cassie sees Nick and Jake throw each other a quick look.

"What?" says Cassie.

Jake squirms. "Well . . . here's the thing. So, my aunt is on the school board, and my cousin Peyton said that they were looking to save some money and there were going to be some cuts."

"They fired Mr. Lewis?" Cassie can't believe this. This is so wrong.

"No! Well, I don't know actually." Jake looks uneasy. "He said they were just talking about cutting some of the things that didn't have a lot of people doing them."

"Like Jazz Lab?" asks Mac.

"Maybe," Jake says, miserably. There is a groan from Mac. "Anything with only a few people doing it."

"Wait," says Quag. "I thought you said Mr. Lewis *quit*."

"That's what they said." Cassie overheard some teachers

talking about it when she took a note down to the office for Ms. Harken. "They shut up as soon as they saw me," says Cassie. "But I definitely heard them say he was quitting. Effective immediately."

"Maybe he heard about the cuts and didn't like it," says Nick. "Maybe he quit because of that."

"We gotta do something. A petition, signatures, stuff like that," says Mac.

"Stuff like that never works, Mac," says Quag.

"Shut up, Quag," says Nick. Nick and Quag sit at the same lunch table every day. Cassie does not know why. They don't like each other. At all.

"Sure it would," says Mac. "If we got a lot of people to sign the petition. They have to listen if there's signatures. We gotta get Mr. Lewis back."

Cassie knows Mac's right. Because if there's no Mr. Lewis, there's no Jazz Lab, and there's no Jazz Ensemble once they get to high school. Not really. Cassie has been looking forward to Jazz Ensemble next year. To keeping what they've built in Jazz Lab going. She doesn't want to lose that.

So yeah. They've got to do something.

JAKE

Super Inconvenient

JAKE HEADS TO THE OFFICE right after lunch. It's both convenient and super inconvenient that his mom works at his school. Convenient because if he forgets his lunch money or phone or anything, he can just stop by the office and borrow whatever he needs. Super inconvenient because if he does one thing a teacher doesn't like, all they have to do is mention it to his mom and, *bam*, instant, real-time mom crackdown. The inconvenience way outweighs the convenience.

But today, it might be convenient. Jake needs to know what happened with Mr. Lewis.

Ms. Acosta, who's the other receptionist at the school, is in the office when Jake gets there, but no Mom. "She's in the conference room," Ms. Acosta says, gesturing down the hall. "Getting ready for a meeting with Mr. Deming and the math faculty. If you hurry, you can catch her."

His mom's alone in the room, hooking up a computer to the smart board, when Jake comes in. "Hey," she says. "How's school?"

Jake does not have time for "How's school." "Did Mr. Lewis quit?" he asks her. "Cassie said he quit."

His mom's face goes instantly sad.

So it's true.

"Why?" Jake wants to know. "Why'd he quit?"

His mom is around the table in two seconds and closing the door. "Jake, I really can't talk to you about that. It's a personnel matter. You know the rule. School stuff stays at school."

"This sucks. Is he coming back? Did he get fired or what?"

"He did not get fired." She fiddles with the back of a chair and sighs. "It's complicated."

Jake's giving her his "All right, so get explaining the complicated, I'm sure I can keep up" look when Mr. Deming sweeps into the room and throws Jake a big smile. "Mr. Cranch. So good to see you." Mom's giving Jake her "Don't you dare bring up that we were talking about what we were talking about" look from behind Deming, so Jake mumbles something and gets out.

But he's mad. What's this whole "It's complicated" thing? That doesn't sound like Lewis just quit.

Jake broods about it all through the last half of the day. He thought there'd be more time before Aunt Scary did whatever evil she'd been planning to do. He didn't think it was like an immediate thing. He's got to talk to his mom about this again. Rule or no rule.

But when he goes back down to the office after school, she's in a meeting, so he finally heads home. The whole walk, all he can think about is Jazz Lab and Jazz Ensemble and Mr. Lewis. Are they just gone? How can they just be gone?

There are three boxes on Jake's driveway with the words *Va Va Va Bloom, Baby* in swirling script across their sides, which is about one "va" and one "baby" more than Jake is up to dealing with today, and then there is that big sign with Aunt Terri's face smirking out from it in the center of the yard. Jake stands and glares at the picture of Aunt Terri like she can see him. How could she do this? After everything he's put up with?

This Two Annoying Aunts Show is quickly swinging from super inconvenient to straight-up disaster.

CASSIE

Chairs

WHEN CASSIE COMES UP to the sound booth after school on Thursday for play rehearsal, Quagmire is already there. As usual. But he's not sitting in Cassie's chair. Definitely not the usual. Cassie is immediately suspicious. He doesn't acknowledge her except for a lazy glance. Turns back to his all-consuming soundboard.

All right. Cassie will give him this: she has not had to teach him one single thing about the soundboard. Either Mr. Saavedra's given him some serious get-up-to-speed training in the last two weeks, or he's been looking everything up online. She suspects online. She's come in a couple of times when he's had a video tutorial up on the laptop screen. He switched screens as soon as he saw her. But she admits that he has not been the washout she thought he would be as soundman. He's pretty good, actually.

Doesn't talk much. Like at all, hardly. Honestly, that's kind of a relief after Chuckie. But he runs the soundboard. Doesn't try to mess with what Cassie's doing with the lights. So it's working out better than she thought.

Still. The chair switch means he's trying to get something.

Usually, Cassie's way ahead of that kind of thing. This time, she knows that it's happening but not *why* it's happening. No idea.

What does a kid like Quagmire want?

She drops her backpack in the corner. Lowers herself into the chair. She has missed this chair. She uses the little lever on the side to adjust the height to fit her perfectly. She doesn't want to give Quagmire one second of satisfaction over the switch. But she can't help kind of swinging the chair side to side once. There's this tiny, second-long quirk to the edge of Quagmire's mouth when he sees her. Might be what passes for a smile in Quagmireland.

Yeah, he wants something.

If there's one thing Cassie has learned from living with her dad, it's that you don't play the games. You see a game, you call it. Saves time. She leans over and knocks lightly on his headphones.

He turns toward her, lurching back a little. It's impossible to turn in that chair without it trying to dump you on the floor. He raises an eyebrow at her. Lifts the earpiece nearest her off his ear.

"What do you want?" Cassie asks him.

"What?" The usual Quagmire glare is back.

"Why'd you give me back my chair? What do you want?"

He glances out the front of the booth. Reaches across the board. Flicks a couple of switches. "Decided I like this one better. Got a problem with that?"

Yeah, right.

He wants something.

QUAGMIRE

What He Wanted

QUAGMIRE DOESN'T KNOW what he wants. Anyway, he knows she won't give him a single thing in exchange for that chair. Not one thing. He respects that.

He hadn't done it for that. He doesn't know why he did it. He just did, okay? Not a big deal. Get over it already.

But something does shift over the next days. Once, Cassie wordlessly hands him a pen when she sees he needs to mark a new square on the board tape. Then, during the tragedy of that long, long flat note in Brendon Carlyle's solo in rehearsal, he holds an Oreo out in the space between them, and she takes it, neither of them taking their eyes from the train wreck on the stage. And when Mandi Elliot, who's come up to do her weekly motto refresh on the whiteboard, screams and starts stomping around the sound booth trying to murder a spider, Cassie's arm shoots out to block Mandi at the exact second that Quag reaches out to gather the spider carefully into his fist and place it high up on a dark shelf in the back, where it can wander through the corridors of old boxes in peace until the end of its days.

And it feels a whole lot like each of those things is something he'd wanted without knowing he'd wanted it.

NICK

Nobody Home

NICK DOESN'T WANT TO TELL the other band kids that he knows where Mr. Lewis lives. Because then they'll want to know why, and he feels funny talking about it. But he does know where Mr. Lewis lives, and he figures the fastest way to find out what's really going on is to just check in with Mr. Lewis. So he stops by the Lewises' house that Friday afternoon, but no one answers the door. And then he stops by twice more over the weekend. But the PennySaver ads from last week are still on the steps, all sogged from the rain, and there isn't a car in the driveway either time. Nick rings the bell again and again, but clearly nobody is home.

And something about that empty house, something about the doorbell ringing through rooms with no one in them, weirds Nick out. Makes him feel like he shouldn't be here. Like he shouldn't come back.

JAKE

Petition

LILY AND CASSIE ARE at the guys' lunch table again today. Jake slides onto the seat across from them. "Something strange is definitely going on," he says. "I tried to talk to my mom about Mr. Lewis this weekend, and she wouldn't tell me anything. At all. She went all thus-saith-the-mom and told me she absolutely could not discuss matters involving the school with me. I mean, 'matters involving the school' are ninety percent of my life, so what's up with that? Then her sisters kept calling about stuff, so that gave her the excuse to avoid talking to me about anything at all."

"You don't think they fired him because he's old, do you?" says Mac. "Because that would be like *discrimination* or something."

"No. She says Mr. Lewis didn't get fired. But something's going on."

"Look," says Cassie. "Whatever it is, we have to stop it. I thought about what Mac said about a petition, and I think it's a good idea. Me and Lily printed one up last night." She unzips her backpack and thunks down a stack of papers with

"SAVE JAZZ LAB" printed across the top. "We get people to sign it and let everyone know that we're not okay with this. That we want Mr. Lewis and Jazz Lab back." There are nods all around the table.

Except from Quag. Quag's shaking his head, and what he says to Cassie is "It's not just about you."

Which does not make Cassie too happy. Nope. If Jake were Quag, he would be taking cover about now because she's turning around and getting right in Quag's face.

"What did you say?" asks Cassie.

But Quag doesn't back down at all. "You're acting like the school board is on some kind of specialized mission to kill Jazz Lab. Think about it. How much money is cutting one little class going to save? If they're going after Jazz Lab, they're probably going after other stuff too."

"Quag's right," says Nick.

Jake looks at Nick. Mac looks at Nick. Cassie looks at Nick. Lily looks at Nick. The world is ending. The world is ending right here in Southton Falls at 11:03 at this lunch table: Nick Finlay just agreed with Quagmire Tiarello.

"He is," says Nick. "I mean, more cuts, more money saved, you know. Jake, didn't your cousin say the school was going after anything that didn't have a lot of people doing it?"

"He did say that," agrees Jake.

"Art club is pretty small," says Cassie.

"Chess club," says Jake.

"Those kids that play the handbells in Ms. Tisbe's room during lunch hour," says Nick.

"Foods class. Or restaurant management. Whatever that little class is called with the kids who are totally wanting to be chefs and stuff," says Jake.

"This *stinks*." Even Mac can't see anything to be cheerful about today. "This whole thing *stinks*. They'll get rid of everything that's fun."

"Just because something's fun doesn't mean we aren't learning stuff," says Lily.

More nods around the table.

Cassie adds *AND STUDENT CLUBS AND ELECTIVES* in red ink to the top of her petition sheet.

"We need something that says why," says Lily. She takes the pen and prints *The things we learn in classes and clubs we choose are important. Please keep them.*

"Good," says Cassie. "So everybody take a couple of petitions and copy what Lily wrote on top and start asking people. Make sure everybody only signs once though. Jake, you take chess club. Nick, art club. I'll get the handbell kids. Lily, foods. Mac, anybody we've missed."

"Got it," says Mac. "Everybody else!" Good call by Cassie. Mac's life specialty is talking to anyone anywhere even without an assignment.

MAC

Disappearing Act

MAC HEADS OVER TO THE TABLE where some of the kids who take wood shop always sit. They weren't on Cassie's list, but "everyone else" is Mac's job. He tells them about Mr. Lewis leaving and the school maybe cutting other small classes and clubs. "So we're getting signatures to ask them not to do it. Wanna sign?" he asks.

"I'll sign," says Sam Armitage, reaching for the paper. "But you're kind of late. They've been cutting stuff for a while."

Mac is confused. "When?" he asks. "What stuff?"

"Lots of stuff," says Sam. "When my brother went to middle school, there was metal shop, and wood shop all year in eighth grade. Now there's only wood shop, and it's only half the year. You got to take some random career survey class the other half of the year."

"That's true," Micah Nichols says. "And when my cousin went to the high school, they used to have a whole auto shop. Their senior year, he and a couple friends rebuilt a Jeep Honcho.

Bodywork, engine work, the whole deal. It was sweet. That's all gone now too."

"By the time my kid sister gets to middle school, there'll be nothing at all, maybe," says Sam. "Which kind of stinks for her, because she'd be better at all that kind of stuff than any of us, but she'll never even get to try it."

WHOA. Mac wonders what else has disappeared that he never even knew about.

NICK

If

THIS IS WHAT NICK NEEDS to know. This is what he thinks about as he lies in bed at night, looking up at the ugly part of his ceiling where there used to be a leak: If Mr. Lewis leaves for good and there's no Jazz Lab, will there still be a Jazz Lab table at lunch?

LILY

Petition

ASKING PEOPLE TO SIGN a petition is hard for Lily, but she told Cassie she'd do it, and she will. She'll do anything to save Jazz Lab. The only person she knows in foods class is Saima Nezami, who wasn't here yesterday, so she needs to talk to other people until she can check in with Saima about who else is in that class. She thinks about asking the people sitting around her in physical science today to sign, but by the time she thinks through what she could say to them, Mr. Byishimo has started the class, and it's too late. And then Jake's already got everyone in English to sign before she even gets there. Mac walks by in the hall waving a stack of petitions, and it looks like he already has pages and pages filled. Lily wants a stack like that.

She follows Ellie Han as she separates from the lunchroom-bound crowd and turns into the biology room. Ellie is nice. She'll sign.

Lily hesitates in the doorway. The lights are out in the

classroom, but in the back of the room are trays and trays of plants on shelves almost as tall as Lily. Lights are suspended over each tray and shine across Ellie's face as she turns her head and checks on a plant. Ellie isn't the only one here. Lily recognizes Cory Franklin, with his round glasses and curly hair, looking at some sort of dial on the side of the shelving. Cory is nice too, so maybe he'll sign. That would be a start.

Ellie is the first to see Lily, and she stops and tucks a strand of hair behind her ear. Cory looks up, and the lenses of his glasses pick up the light in a way that turns them gold, and Lily can't see his eyes anymore. They stand looking at each other across the darkened room.

"The little tomatoes are ready," says Cory in his soft voice. Lily has only heard Cory ever talk before when he was called on by a teacher. But here Cory's quiet voice seems right, like he is trying not to break the spell of the quiet plants or something.

"Come see," says Ellie, gesturing toward Lily. Lily makes her way through the silent desks and chairs until she's standing next to Ellie and Cory. Cory points at a huge, sprawling plant hanging down from the top tray. It's covered with little round balls that look like red beads.

"What are those?" Lily asks.

"They're tomatoes!" says Ellie. "Here." She reaches out

and picks ten or so of the tiny things off the plant and then, cupping them in her palm, turns to Lily. They are no bigger than Lily's pinkie nail, and some have green stems shaped like stars clinging to them. How can these be tomatoes? They're so little. Ellie pulls off one of the stars and drops the tiny globe into her mouth. She holds her hand out to Lily. "Try one."

Lily does. A burst of sweet and sour hits her tongue. "They *are* tomatoes," she says. "I didn't know tomatoes could be this small."

Ellie grins and eats the rest of the handful. "They're even better if you eat a bunch at once," she says.

"Or put them with some of the lettuce and eat them that way." Cory has pulled a leaf off one of the plants and piled a few of the tiny tomatoes inside. He hands it to Lily.

It's really beautiful. The lettuce leaf is ruffled and flecked with deep purple, and the tomatoes glisten red inside the cupped leaf.

"How do I eat it?" Lily asks.

"Any way you want to," says Ellie, picking a leaf for herself, folding it around a few tomatoes, and popping it in her mouth.

Lily folds her leaf like Ellie did and bites into it. It's crisp, sweet, tangy, bitter, everything, in one little package.

"Good, huh?" says Ellie. "It's a Cory invention. Portable salad. No forks."

Cory ducks his head, but Lily can tell he's smiling. The air around them smells fresh and sweet. Tucked away in this empty biology room, Lily has found a quiet, light-bathed kingdom of tiny tomatoes. She hates to even bring up the subject of the petition. It's so peaceful here.

She says it out loud. "It's peaceful here."

Cory nods. "We're only supposed to come in here quick to check the pumps and test the acidity of the growing solution, but sometimes I stay for a while. The cafeteria can be a bit much." Lily knows how he feels. The noise in the halls, the clamor of the lunchroom, everyone talking at the same time. It can feel like she has to brace herself against it some days.

"Are you doing this for a class?" Lily asks.

"No," says Ellie. "It's hydroponics club. We meet every Tuesday after school. Sometimes more often if we have to harvest stuff. But last year our pump burned out, and no one knew for a week, and a bunch of stuff died, so now we have teams check on it every day just to make sure."

So Lily has to tell them about the petition. Because maybe they're one of the groups that would get shut down. When she finishes telling them, both Ellie and Cory are shaking their heads. "It took us two years to get this whole system set up right," says Cory. "They can't get rid of it just when we got it working. And we've been giving all the lettuce to the food pantry."

"Give me one of the petitions," says Ellie. "We'll get everybody in hydroponics club to sign."

MAC

You Kidding Me?

LEWIS HASN'T BEEN IN SCHOOL for three classes now. STINKS. First day Lewis wasn't here, some sub — tall dude with a beard — came and passed out multiple-choice worksheets on Who's Who in American Jazz and Jazz Tunes You Might Know. Then, Tuesday, some lady who straight-up said she had no music experience came. She told them to do homework for other classes during that hour. Now the bearded sub is back, gives them another worksheet — What Is Swing? — then sits in the desk in the corner that Mr. Lewis never bothered with and gets out his phone.

The whole class is looking at each other like, "You KIDDING me?" and SCHLIP, SCHLOOP, all the fun that was in that class rushes right out the window.

Cassie's like, "Hey, our spring concert is coming up in two weeks. We've got to get ready. Can't we do that instead?"

The guy shrugs. He's like, "As long as you keep things orderly."

ORDERLY?

They try to play. Mac tries to make the piano swing with the bass. Tries to get that clarinet and sax and trumpet talking to each other. It's sad city times twelve. They miss Mr. Lewis. It's not that they can't play. They can all play. It's that, somehow, without Mr. Lewis, it doesn't feel like PLAY anymore.

MAC

Petition

SAM AND MICAH WANT MORE shop stuff added back. Elena Lapointe wants to know why they don't teach French in the middle school anymore. The girls from the tennis team want to know why football has two teams and got new uniforms last year, even though their old ones were perfectly fine, but the tennis team can't even get nets that don't have big holes in them or the cracks in the courts fixed. "There's a tree growing up through the middle of one of the courts this year," says Mady Chansky. "We named him Bert, and we just play around him, but actually it's kind of a pain." Some kids want to start a futsal league but got told the gym space was needed for the "traditional sports." The environmental club kids want the cafeteria to stop using plastic utensils and straws. Ellie Han and a bunch of other kids who grow lettuce or something for the food pantry just want to keep growing lettuce.

Seems like everybody's got a story for him, and Mac keeps adding notes down the sides of the petitions, trying to tell those stories to someone who will listen.

LILY

Lunch Table

IT USED TO BE THAT Lily's lunch table was just Lily and Cassie, sitting at the end of the table farthest from the door. There's a pillar there, and somehow, even with so many kids in the room during lunchtime, being tucked behind the pillar made it feel like it was a little apart—just the two of them. A safe spot in a long day.

And then they moved over to the boys' table so they could work together on the petition and stuff, and Lily gets why they need to be here, but sometimes she misses their old table. Misses how Cassie would show her the new pictures and texts her Aunt Becca was always sending. Misses how a quick look between her and Cassie was all they needed to say almost anything. The boys are funny and nice, but she has to think about what she wants to say now, and she never knows what will happen at lunch these days. Stuff is happening all the time.

Today, with even more people from this club or that class gathered around the lunch table with them, and everyone talking about things they want and things they don't want to lose and what should go on the petition and who they can get to sign it, part of her feels like it's too much. Part of her wishes that she and Cassie were back behind their pillar, safe. But another part of her thinks about that sweet little world she discovered in the back of the biology room last Tuesday, with the soft smells and soft lights and soft voices, and she wonders if all these kids gathered around this table have been making their own little worlds like that one and like the one the Jazz Lab kids made with Mr. Lewis. And if they have, then it's worth coming out from behind the pillar, even if it's kind of hard. It feels important. It feels like those are worlds worth saving if they can.

CASSIE

What Cassie Sees

"WANT A RIDE TO SCHOOL?" Cassie's dad asks, standing at the door, tossing his keys. And she says yes. Because the printer didn't work right this morning while she was trying to print out more petitions. Took her a superlong time to fix. It's 7:42. She is definitely going to be late unless she gets a ride.

Cassie hates being late. Also, she has seventy-two pounds of homework in her backpack and it's raining. So, yes, she wants a ride.

They're driving down Laurel with the *fwush, thump* of the truck's wipers and the hiss of the tires on the wet asphalt being the only sounds. Neither of them wants to try a conversation. Everything starts a fight lately. The light turns red.

Wonderful. They're cutting it close as it is.

But as they're sitting at the stoplight, Cassie sees Quagmire Tiarello come out of a little house farther down the street. Wow. He is definitely going to be late. Except he isn't even turning toward school. He's coming this way. Opens up a cartoony umbrella that is so not him. Turns around to wait for someone coming out of the house. A woman in a green raincoat. He holds the umbrella over her head. They both walk toward the Metrobus stop.

Cassie notices all this. But the thing she really notices is that he's different than usual. Just different. Like, he's with this kind of older lady—his mom? Or his grandma maybe? Hard to tell. One of those ladies with the dyed red hair that doesn't look good on older ladies but they can't seem to give up on. She has a face that looks like life's been hard. Tough to tell her age.

But the strange thing, the strangest thing, is that Cassie gets the sense that Quagmire's the adult here. Not sure why. Okay, he's the one holding the umbrella. He's got her big purse tucked under his arm. What's up with that?

Then, when they're partway to the bus stop, he hands over the umbrella for a minute and stoops down and ties her shoe. It's weird. Just kind of off in some way. Like he's steering her to the bus stop. Like you'd see a mom steer a little kid who might go wandering into the street without supervision. Or forget where they were going if the mom weren't there.

The light changes to green. The truck turns left and moves on. But the rest of the way to school, as the rain streaks down her window, all Cassie can see in her mind is Quagmire Tiarello standing on a street corner next to a tired, old woman, holding an umbrella printed with orange and pink kittens over her head.

QUAGMIRE

Late

DEMING IS IN THE FRONT OFFICE when Quagmire finally gets to school. Perfect. Couldn't start the day better. And, of course, Deming feels like he has to have a conversation.

"Sleeping in again, I see, Mr. Tiarello," he says, arms folded.

If Quag had known he was going to have to hear this, he wouldn't have come in at all, would have just gotten his mom on the bus and gone back to the house. Caught up on his sleep. Played some video games. What's the point?

Deming clasps his hands behind his back and rocks on the heels of those perfect, shiny black lace-ups, and Quagmire wants to climb over the counter and knock him down. Because of all the things he hates about Deming, the thing he hates most is that Deming'll say stuff like "Sleeping in again," without ever imagining that it could be something else.

LILY

Why?

IT'S SO SAD NOW. The too-quiet music hall. The band room that feels too big even with all of them in it. Lily doesn't like coming down here every Tuesday and Thursday anymore. It used to be her favorite thing.

But now. No more Mac dancing behind the piano. No more coming in to a huge, friendly argument between Jake and Mac over an arrangement they're working on. No more of Nick sometimes playing a fanfare when someone comes through the door.

They still try to play. Cassie makes sure of that. They have only three more practices before spring concert, and it's like she won't give the substitute the satisfaction of seeing they can't do it by themselves, won't give him an excuse to hand out some make-work worksheet and call it music class. But it's hard.

Not hard like it used to be with difficult music and learning things they never knew about before. A different kind of hard. Today, while Lily was playing an arrangement of "Sticks" that Mac and Mr. Lewis had written up for them, she looked over to where Mr. Lewis should have been playing the drums, and her throat ached so bad that she just let her bass go quiet under her hands. And then, one by one, the others dropped out too, until they were all sitting silently, all sad in that sad, sad room.

Here's what Lily doesn't understand. Even if Mr. Lewis is mad that the school board is going to cut Jazz Lab like Jake says they're going to, shouldn't he have stayed here with them until it happened? Shouldn't he have helped them try to save it?

He shouldn't have left like that. He shouldn't have left them to figure this out on their own. Even if it made him sad like it's making them sad. They should have all played through together.

Why would he do that? Why did he leave them?

CASSIE

Petition

CASSIE'S PRETTY PROUD OF the collection of petitions she's got in her arms. She called Aunt Becca to tell her about what they were doing, and Aunt Bec asked her to email a petition to her so she could sign it and email it back. So that's in the pile. And then about everybody they asked in the school signed. Even a few teachers. Maybe they could have got more people if they had more time, but they got a lot. It's a pretty impressive stack of papers, and Cassie's tied it up with some bright yellow cord from Aunt Becca's workshop so that nobody could miss it. And now she and the rest of Jazz Lab are taking the petition over to the office.

But when they get into the office, neither receptionist is at her desk. Cassie, Lily, Jake, Nick, and Mac all kind of clump in front of the counter. "Where is everybody?" says Jake. "Somebody's always supposed to be here." But somebody isn't, and there's no bell to ring like you do at the dry cleaners or anything, so they all just stand, awkwardly waiting.

Jake fishes out his phone and texts his mom. But it's the other receptionist, Ms. Acosta, who finally comes around the corner and sees them standing there. "Oh!" she says. "Sorry. How long have you been here?" She slides into her desk. "What can I do for you?"

"We want to see Mr. Deming," says Cassie.

"He's in a meeting with student council right now," says Ms. Acosta. "Can I give him a message?"

"Can we just wait?" Cassie wants to deliver the petition right to Principal Deming.

"Well, he'll be in there for the next forty or so minutes. And then he's got a meeting with some parents," says Ms. Acosta. "And don't all of you need to be in class right now?"

"We're *here* because of class," says Mac. "We're here because of Jazz Lab and Mr. Lewis. We've got a *petition*."

Ms. Acosta gets a strange, almost embarrassed, look on her face at the mention of Mr. Lewis. Cassie doesn't quite understand that look. But Ms. Acosta gets up and comes out from behind the counter. "Listen," she says. "I would be happy to deliver that petition to Mr. Deming for you. I can get it right on his desk where he'll see it. I promise." Her face looks gentle and sad, and somehow it makes Cassie hand the stack of petitions over to her. "Do you want to send a message along with the petition?" Ms. Acosta asks.

"Yes," says Cassie. "We want Jazz Lab and Mr. Lewis back. And we've been talking to a lot of the kids in the other electives and clubs, and they all want to keep their stuff too."

Ms. Acosta looks puzzled but pulls a memo pad across the counter, and Cassie can see that she's writing down exactly what Cassie said.

"And can I put down who is bringing this petition? In case Mr. Deming has questions?" She's already written *Jake Cranch*, but Cassie runs through the rest of their names, and Ms. Acosta writes them.

"Us, but also everybody that signed the petition," adds Cassie.

"Of course," says Ms. Acosta. "Of course. I'll get this to him as soon as he's out of his meetings. And let me write you up hall passes for your next class. You're going to be a few minutes late, I think."

They head out down the hall, and Mac is high-fiving people. "Did you *see* how many signatures were in that stack?" he says. But Cassie is wondering if they should have waited and given the petition straight to Principal Deming. And she's wondering what was up with the way Ms. Acosta went all strange when they mentioned Mr. Lewis.

QUAGMIRE

Petition

AT THE LUNCH TABLE YESTERDAY, the Jazz Lab kids were all excited about the petition they'd taken down to the office. Quag didn't get it. So they got a bunch of people to sign a paper that said what they wanted. Perfect. And now exactly nothing at all was going to change.

But they thought it was a big deal. Only Cassie seemed a little out of the celebration, like she was thinking something over. Cassie's smart. She probably knows better. Quag doesn't get why she bothered.

Today, the band kids seem more dialed down. Like they're surprised Deming hasn't appeared and begged on bended knee to restore everything they hold dear. Seriously. Has no one else been paying any attention at all the last eight years? Should not be a surprise.

No one at the table is talking much, and Cassie's doodling stuff along the margins of her notebook. A cowboy boot. A saxophone. A string of notes. Over Cassie's shoulder, Quagmire sees a group of five kids steaming through the cafeteria toward their table. Cassie doesn't notice them until Tipton Martinkus comes up on her left and slams a big stack of paper wrapped up in some eye-bending, crime-tape-yellow rope or something onto the table. Cassie jumps and then looks up at Tipton. "Where did you get this?" Cassie asks.

Quag leans over to see what it is. It's the petition.

"Garbage," says Tipton. "We found it in the garbage!"

"Not even the recycling bin," adds Elijah Pelkey, as if that's somehow relevant.

"Why was it in the garbage?" says Cassie.

"You tell me," says Tipton, all seventy short and spindly pounds of her looking like she's ready to pummel someone. "Mr. Justus is letting us do a survey of everything that gets thrown away in a week in this school for environmental club, and today when we went down there before he took everything out to the dumpster, this was in the garbage. Dev's the one who found it. He noticed the red writing on the top from when he signed it."

Mac's eyes are huge. "Do you think Ms. Acosta just chucked it?"

"No way," says Jake. "No way. She's friends with my mom. She isn't like that. If she said she would put it on Mr. Deming's desk, she put it on Mr. Deming's desk."

Cassie is running her finger over the yellow cord. "He didn't even unwrap it?" She slides a nail along the length of cord and then around the knot holding it together in the middle, as if convincing herself that this is really the package she left in the office yesterday. "He didn't even unwrap it."

"So he didn't even read it," adds Lily.

CASSIE

Over His Head

HE DIDN'T EVEN READ IT. All that work, all those kids who signed, and he didn't even look at what they had to say.

"Here come the junior suits," says Quag. "Hide the petition."

Cassie slides the bedraggled papers under her notebook. Gina Yoon and Dante Lake, student body president and vice president, are heading across the cafeteria toward them. Cassie's not sure why it even matters at this point. This whole thing is a disaster already. But Gina and Dante seem pretty tight with Principal Deming, sitting up on the stage with him during assemblies and meeting in his office every week, so Quag's probably right about keeping them out of this.

"Hi," says Gina, moving to the end of the table next to Cassie. "We'd like to help with the petition."

So much for keeping them out of this.

"What petition?" says Quag.

Gina gives him a sharp look. "We're not stupid, Quagmire. We know there's been a petition circulating all week to ask the school not to cut the small classes and clubs. And we heard Ms. Acosta talking to Mr. Deming about it right after student council yesterday, so it's obviously a thing."

"See, I told you Ms. Acosta wasn't the one who threw it in the garbage," says Jake.

"It ended up in the garbage?" Dante asks.

Gina and Dante exchange a glance and apparently come to some decision. "Remember when Dante and I ran for office at the end of last year?" says Gina. "Remember our fifteen-point platform with all the changes we wanted to make?" Cassie does remember. It was actually pretty cool. Specific things that needed to change instead of the usual "Vote for me, I'm popular" stuff. Cassie voted for Gina and Dante. She nods.

"So then what's happened with all that?" Gina asks.

Kind of an embarrassing question for her to ask. Because now that Cassie's thinking about it, she can't remember a single thing on that list that they've actually done.

"Nothing," says Quag. Trust Quag to say it out loud.

"Exactly," says Gina.

"We got shut down," says Dante.

"Every week, we go into student government, and he's got some busywork he wants us to get through before we can get to the stuff we want to do," says Gina. "And when we complain that we're never working on the things we think are important, he'll pretend something is going to change and then come up with some reason why it can't. *And* we get trotted out at every event, every announcement of something we didn't come up with, like these are *our* ideas."

"We're getting used," says Dante. "But our parents are like, 'Sometimes change is hard—just keep trying.' But nothing is changing. Nothing. You've got something started. We want to help."

Cassie slides the petition out from under her notebook and hands it to Gina. "Well, what we got started somehow ended up in the trash can. Environmental club found it," says Cassie, gesturing toward Tipton and her friends, who are gathered around the table listening in, "or we wouldn't have even known."

Gina and Dante share another one of their communicating-without-saying-anything looks. "You have to go over Deming's head," says Gina. "To the school board."

"How do we even do that?" asks Nick.

"Take the petition to their meeting," says Dante. "Wouldn't hurt at all if we could get some parents involved too. Kind of late notice though."

"When's their next meeting?" asks Cassie.

"Well," says Gina, "that's the thing. It's tonight."

CASSIE

Seriously?

"OKAY, LISTEN UP." CASSIE FOLDS her notebook over to a blank page. "New plan. We're taking the petition straight to the school board."

"Got it," says Nick. The other kids around the table nod.

"What time's the school board meeting?" Cassie asks Gina.

"Seven," says Lily. She slides her phone to the middle of the table. "Here's the agenda I found on the school website."

Cassie turns the phone so she can see. "They're talking about next year's budget tonight."

"This is *bogus!*" Mac's scowling at everyone at the table. "They threw them in the *garbage?*" It's like he still can't believe it happened.

It happened.

"I can't come tonight," says Jake.

"Why not?" asks Mac. "I bet my mom can give you a ride if your mom's busy."

Jake squirms. Doesn't want to talk about it. Obviously.

But Mac isn't backing off. "We'll pick you up on the way."

"No, my aunt's wedding rehearsal is tonight," Jake says. "I got to go to it."

"I thought your aunt was going to be at the school board thing," says Nick.

"Different aunt," says Jake.

"How many aunts you got?" says Nick.

"Two too many. The school board aunt is Aunt Terri. The one that's getting married is Aunt Cece."

"Your Aunt Cece is getting married *again?*" asks Mac.

Jake rolls his eyes.

But Cassie's feeling something wash over her that's exactly like what she always imagined doom would feel like. "Wait," she says. "What's your aunt's name again?"

"Which one?" asks Jake.

"The getting-married one."

"Cece," says Jake.

Cassie tips her head to the side. Okay. Maybe they're okay. "Cece, not Celia?" She wants to make sure.

"Well, her real name is Celia, but everybody calls her Cece."

Not everybody.

"Celia Stott?" Cassie asks.

"Yeah." Jake's giving her a confused look. Like he knows something is off but can't quite figure it out.

No.

No, no, no. Please, no. This is not happening.

"What's the name of the guy she's marrying?" Cassie feels weirdly calm for someone hurtling toward disaster.

"I dunno. Bob. Rob. Something like that."

Yeah. Something like that. "Rob Byzinski?"

Cassie has never thought of the expression "eyes popping out of your head" as anything but exaggeration. Until this moment. Jake's eyes do this huge, cartoonish bulge as he realizes that Cassie and he are mere days away from the train wreck of becoming cousins. Or whatever they'll become. Cassie has a sudden creepy vision of two eyeballs rolling across the table, bouncing over the cafeteria floor, and disappearing down the main stairway to finally roll to a stop in some dusty corner near the furnace room.

Doesn't happen, luckily. But Jake turns this amazing green-tinged white. Followed by a blooming red.

Awkward moment of the century.

Seriously? This is too weird. Being in Jazz Lab together. Fine. Being friends at school. Fine. But having her never-know-what's-going-to-happen-next dad married to Jake's flaky Aunt Cece?

One by one, everybody at the table catches on. Responds in their typical way. Lily, worried frown. Mac, huge grin. Quag, sly smirk. Nick, mild dismay. Even Gina and Dante and Tipton look a little amused.

Unreal. Like Cassie doesn't have enough problems right now.

JAKE

Seriously?

JAKE WAITS UNTIL HE AND HIS MOM are sitting down for an early dinner to bring it up. "Did you know about the Cassie thing?" he asks her.

She lifts her eyebrows. Steam rises off the rigatoni.

"The Cassie thing?" she asks.

"Did you know about it?"

His mom raises her hands. "Jake, I don't even know what you're talking about."

Fine. He will spell it out. "Did you know that the guy that Aunt Cece is marrying this Saturday is Cassie Byzinski's dad?" He can see from her expression that she did know about that. Which makes him even madder.

"Were you not going to tell me?"

"I thought you knew. And I didn't think it was that big of a deal. Cassie is a very nice girl."

That is not the point. "Mom, you know this is going to be a disaster, right? You know Aunt Cece is going to ruin my friend's life, right?"

"What an awful thing to say."

Jake pushes his chair back. Just because something is an awful thing to say doesn't mean it isn't true. Doesn't mean they haven't seen this story roll out before. Because Aunt Cece loves this getting-married-as-a-hobby thing, but it never lasts. Never. And Jake can't really see her as the good stepmom type. Jake gives the marriage a year, year and a half max, and then the whole thing will go up in flames like it always does, and Cassie will be caught in the middle of that. "This is just setting Cassie up for a whole bunch of drama she doesn't need."

Jake picks up his plate. If his mom's not going to talk to him about anything that has to do with school or Mr. Lewis, and she's not going to listen to anything that has to do with family, then what is the point of even being down here? He's going to go eat in his room. "It's not okay, Mom. It's really not."

CASSIE

Prior Engagement

"NO CAN DO, CASSAROONI," says her dad when Cassie asks him to go to tonight's school board meeting. "Prior engagement. Wedding rehearsal," he says. Laughs. Because that's hilarious.

But Cassie knows. He wouldn't show up even if he had the night free. Because her dad, Rob Byzinski, likes people to like him. Always. Cassie thinks he senses that something like a school board talking about budget cuts will be immune to his let's-throw-charm-on-that life technique.

"You can't go either, Cass," he says. "You're supposed to be at the wedding rehearsal tonight too."

First Cassie has heard of that. She had to find out about this rehearsal in front of the whole lunch table at school. Because he never asks. Not in second grade when he signed her up for boxing lessons because he thought it would be cute to have a tough little boxer daughter. Not when he moved them to LA. Not when he moved them to Pennsylvania. Not when he moved them to Ohio. To Georgia. To New Jersey.

Wouldn't surprise Cassie if someday her dad came home and said, "Hey, Cass! You're gonna love this. I've signed us up to be a father-daughter team on a new reality show where we do competitive hot dog eating in each of the seven continents. We'll win modeling contracts if we come in first. We leave tomorrow. Won't that be fun?"

Then if she said, "No, Father. That does not sound like fun. I loathe hot dogs. I don't want to grow up to be a human clothes rack," he'd act all hurt. Like this was something she'd been begging to do since she was four, and now that he's sacrificed by quitting his latest job so they can do it, Cassie has changed her mind. Backed out. Now what's he supposed to tell his fantasy football buddies? They've already got a pool going on whether he and Cassie will take first prize.

Cassie gets tired of him not asking. And she gets tired of being the kid whose dad skips parent night and doesn't show up for her concerts. She doesn't even know why she bothered to ask him to come to the school board meeting. It was never going to happen.

Well, neither is the wedding rehearsal. "Sorry," Cassie says. "Prior engagement."

MAC

Nope

"PUT IT ON THE LIST for family meeting, Mac," says his mom, unloading some groceries into the freezer.

"That'll be too late!" Family meeting only happens on the second Sunday of the month.

"I'm sure there's got to be some misunderstanding," says Mac's mom.

"How is there a MISUNDERSTANDING? The stuff was in the GARBAGE! So we have to go to the school board meeting TONIGHT!" Mac tries again. "Mom, this is important."

"Everything's important this week, Mac. Your dad's out of town, so I'm already trying to run a two-parent schedule with only one parent. I'll look into this situation at the school, but I have a meeting that I'm leading in Syracuse tonight, and I can't leave everyone in the lurch to go to a different meeting that you just told me about." She shoves a stack of folders into her bag. "Mari's in charge tonight, so help out. And don't let the twins eat junk, okay?" And she's sweeping out the door.

And now Mac's starting to get what it's like when people aren't listening to you.

JAKE

Sneaking Out

"HIS VEST IS ALL BAGGY, Audrey," says Aunt Cece. "Why didn't you get it altered?" Aunt Cece is buzzing around in full event-planner mode. She is completely oblivious to the fact that Jake isn't real happy with her. And that Jake and his mom aren't real happy with each other after their dinner discussion earlier. Aunt Cece gets paid to plan corporate trade shows, but there is nothing she likes better than planning a wedding—particularly her own—so nothing else exists right now. If there is a crooked tablecloth anywhere in this building, Jake feels for it.

Aunt Cece sighs. "Never mind. Just pin the vest up. And, Jake, pull up your socks."

Mom also sighs, but she takes the box of wicked-long pins that Cece hands her and starts poking them into Jake's vest. Jake does not pull up his stupid socks. He does not complain about the fact that four-inch-long instruments capable of inflicting puncture wounds are being inserted into an article of clothing that is only a millimeter from his skin and vital organs. He does not ask why Aunt Scary is excused from this rehearsal, but he is not. He does not say a word.

But he does make a decision. He pulls out his phone and, holding it close to his offending vest, texts Mac. He's not going to spend two hours immersed in the stupidity of practicing walking in a straight line down an aisle. He's going to that school board meeting with his friends.

When Mac finally texts that he's here, Jake glides carefully away from the current site of disaster (they've moved on from the baggy vest to ribbons on some table that don't quite match with something else on the table and are apparently going to bring on the end of all known civilizations), and he's out in the hall. He ditches his vest in a large fancy vase sitting on a small fancy table and heads toward the main entrance. He avoids eye contact with the lady with the severe bun sitting behind the counter in the foyer of the events center.

Mac's minivan is sitting at the curb, and Mac slides the door open from the inside. Then Jake's in and they're off.

Mac's sister, Mari, is driving, and the four-year-old twins are in the back in booster seats. "Jakey," they chorus, and reach out hands that seem to have been in recent close contact with some Flavor Blasted Goldfish. Jake evades the hands. He knows not to be taken in by the cute little-kid smiles.

These twins are slightly evil. And they have zero sense of

personal space. Which he is reminded of every time he plays video games at Mac's house. You might be trying to fight off aliens or rogue agents or an army of zombies, and you will suddenly find yourself with a four-year-old clamped to your head, or braiding your hair, or trying to put some sort of glitter gloss on you. Mac is pretty good at ignoring all that and playing on, but Jake finds it a little disturbing. Because glitter gloss. Also, the twins sing, a lot.

"Buckle," Mari says to Jake, and he does, because Mari is not someone you mess with. Jake played volleyball with Mac's family once, and he was on Mari's team. Which was great because it was kind of like being on the same team as a living highlight reel. Jake swears there was this one time when she actually jumped in slow motion. He can still remember her rising slowly up and up and up and blocking out the sun as she spiked the ball. But it was also terrifying, because if he let a ball drop on the grass in front of his feet, she would turn and look at him like she was thinking of putting his liver in a frying pan and eating it. Jake only let that first ball fall untried-for, but every time he sees her, he still gets a pain where he thinks she would have made the incision.

Mac adores her though. To be fair, Mac is better at volleyball than Jake is, so she's nicer to Mac.

Mari's pulling her black hair into a ponytail and wrapping it all up with a red cloth tie she has on her wrist, and then she shakes her head and pulls out into traffic. A heavy silence falls in the car. Jake tries not to breathe too loud.

When they're about two blocks from the school, he realizes that he still has those super-embarrassing wedding socks on. He slides one foot over between the door and his seat and tries to slip off his left dress shoe and the sock without anyone noticing.

"What are you doing?" asks one of the twins.

Jake struggles with the sock. Mac is giving him a "Dude, what the heck?" look. Jake pivots to try to get the other foot over between the door and seat to slip that sock off. Mari starts watching him in the rearview mirror. He wads the socks up in his hand and stuffs them into his pants pocket. When he slides his shoes back on, his bare feet feel all slitchy in his shoes. Mac is staring at him. If Mari spends any more time glaring at him in that mirror, she's going to crash this car into a tree.

They pull up to the administration offices. Nick and Lily and Cassie are already there, sitting on a bench by the side of the building. Lily has the petition papers in her arms. Cassie carries a big poster board that says SAVE THE ARTS FROM THE AXE. She looks ready to take down whoever gets in her way. This should be fun. If Jake does not get killed by Mom or Aunt Cece or Aunt Scary, he will probably die in some Cassie-induced mob trampling by enraged school board members.

"Interesting," says Mari, leaning across the passenger seat to look out at Cassie. "This is for social studies, huh?" And she gives Mac a piercing look that he evades by sliding the door open and exiting stage right. Jake scrambles to follow, but the cuff of his dress pants gets caught on some weird lever thing next to his seat, and he's trying to get out the door, but his left leg is not cooperating and is apparently planning instead on remaining permanently attached to his seat.

Mari pins him with this evil, one-eyebrow-arched glare that says if he does not get out of here within two seconds, she will put the car in gear and drag him behind with his head bouncing on the pavement. The twins stretch out their orange-stained hands and shriek his name.

For a minute, Jake thinks he's going to pass out. But then there is a ripping sound, and he stumbles from the car. He is probably going to relive this moment in dreams for the next three months.

"What happened to you?" says Cassie, looking at his ripped pant leg and bare ankles. "Never mind. No time. I made us all posters. Let's go."

CASSIE

What Adults Say

HERE'S WHAT ADULTS SAY when they aren't planning on listening to you.

Parent version:

Stop overthinking everything.

What is your problem? It'll be fine.

Quit worrying. You'll like her/the new house/the new school/the new whatever.

School board version:

Thank you for the interest you're clearly taking in your education. We're always delighted to have young people attend these meetings. We understand your concerns, and we have not made any final budget decisions, but the intricacies of state tax law and school financing sometimes force us to make difficult choices.

JAKE

Two-Aunt Blues

JAKE'S MOM IS ÜBER UNHAPPY by the time she picks him up after the school board meeting. Aunt Terri must have texted her, because his mom's pulling into the parking lot when Jake comes out the door, and he sure didn't call her. She gives him a look that makes him decide that the back seat is a way better option than shotgun, where she could make continued eye contact.

She's apparently still on the phone with Aunt Terri, who gives her an earful as she drives. Or at least Jake's pretty sure that's what's happening. His mom turned off speakerphone as soon as Aunt Terri started in with the "never been so humiliated in all my life, my own nephew showing up at the school board meeting trying to make me look like this insensitive, art-hating hatchet woman" stuff. Jake's mom listens to a one-sided barrage for several blocks, and she puts Aunt Scary on hold only when Aunt Cece calls to complain about them missing most of the rehearsal. Apparently, Rob made some comment about runaway ushers, and then Cece went off on him about at least her daughter wasn't missing, and there was a whole thing. His mom's scrambling for the speakerphone button after that little story too. And the only thing in this whole stupid evening that's gone right is that his mom says, "Cece, I hardly think you having a fight is really Jake's fault," but even though his mom stuck up for him on that one point, Jake knows she is still going to have lots to say to him just as soon as she gets off the phone with her sisters. Under the streetlights, Jake can see the tight line of his mom's jaw as she talks. That line means someone's in for it. Pretty good guess who that someone is going to be, and he's sitting in the back seat of this car.

He wishes, just once, that she would tell her sisters to shut up. That she didn't have to be the good sister, the always-listening ear. Doesn't she get sick of it? Doesn't she ever want to let this stuff go to voicemail and then delete the messages without even listening to them?

And how come she can listen to all this stuff from her sisters, but she can't listen to him about something that really matters to him, something he might be losing?

It's started to rain. Drops streak back against the glass. The whole world's sinking into a wet gray as the sun sets. The edge of the poster board sign pokes Jake in the arm, and he can feel the wad of his stupid socks still in his pocket. He rolls the window down. A fine mist blows on his face. The tires sound sticky against the wet pavement.

He pulls the socks out of his pocket and holds them between his thumb and finger. They ripple and snap in the damp air. He watches them turn yellow, then pink, yellow, then pink as the car passes under the blinking light in front of Foster's Fresh Eats.

And Jake opens his fingers and lets the socks go.

"Jacob Cranch," says his mom, lowering her cell phone from her ear. "You did *not* just throw something out of the car, did you?"

It's going to be a long night.

JAKE

War

THE MOOD AT THE LUNCH TABLE today is bru-
tal. When Jake sits down, Mac's got his head on his arms.
And when Nick says something about how people are blind
for about forty minutes every day because of something called
saccadic masking and Quag says, "No one cares, Nick," really
no one does. Everyone's too depressed.

But when Cassie comes stalking across the lunchroom, it's
clear that she has not gone the depression route. She slams her
books down on the table.

"They did not listen to us at all last night," she says.

"Nope," says Jake.

"They did that super-polite pretending-to-listen thing," says
Lily quietly, sliding in next to Cassie.

"Yep," says Mac.

Quag sits across from Jake, crushing Cheeto after Cheeto
into piles of orange dust with his thumbs. He wasn't even there
last night, but Quag's in a bad mood as often as he's in a good
one, so he's fitting right in today.

"I hate that!" Cassie drums her fists on the table, making the Cheeto dust bounce. "I hate it! It's like they think we're too stupid to know what's going on. Like they think they can just pat us on the head, and we'll go away!"

It's true. Jake's noticed it too. A lot of adults think kids are idiots. They think they're being all sneaky and that if they say something in a fancy way, no one will see what they're up to.

Not the case.

"This is definitely why Mr. Lewis quit," Jake says. "It was like a protest against the stupidity of bureaucracy."

"Well, we should back him up," says Cassie. "We should do our own protest."

"How?" Nick says. "We did a petition, and Deming didn't even care. We went to the school board meeting and talked to them, and they didn't care again."

This is also true. For the whole ridiculous, long meeting last night, all the people on the school board talked about was test scores. They should have just passed out bubble sheets at the door. Everything was about "return on investment." Which programs provided it, which didn't. Way too much talk about "core programs that support test scores" and "fiscal responsibility." Translation: Anything that doesn't show up on the state tests is not important. Anything that isn't boring is not important. Music, art, shop classes, clubs—not important.

The school board left a whole ten minutes for "public

comment," and then some guy with a big belly in an orange T-shirt who thought the school was buying too many buses took up more than that. So by the time the board called on the middle school kids, crowded together in the last row, most everybody in the room just wanted to go home. Except Aunt Terri, who apparently first wanted to burn multiple smoking laser holes through Jake's face with her eyes and then go home.

Cassie still gave a great speech—"Preparing us for life isn't the same as preparing us for some test," and "Teachers who teach us how to learn for ourselves are the best teachers, even if they teach a subject that's not on your list"—while the rest of Jazz Lab stood kind of awkwardly behind her at the front of the room. And the board members clapped politely, but they wouldn't make eye contact, and you could totally see the writing on the wall. They weren't going to listen. They were going to take down Jazz Lab and a whole bunch of other stuff. Jazz Lab not being a core program that supports test scores and all.

So it makes sense that they're depressed today.

Lily reaches across and rubs Cassie's neck and Cassie relaxes a little. But not much.

"You know what?" says Lily. "We have to do something that they can't ignore." And Jake's surprised to hear *Lily* say that. And, at the same time, he realizes she's right. They *do* have to do something no one can ignore.

Mac sits up and brings both his palms down—BOOM—on the table. People at nearby lunch tables swivel to look at him, but Mac doesn't care. He has his "I am a genius" look on. "The concert," he says. "Spring concert is next Thursday. We take it over."

Cassie gives him a sharp look. "Take it over how?" she asks.

"We play last, right? Jazz Lab always plays last. We're like the finale. So instead of playing, we come in and protest. Maybe don't play. Maybe just stand there with pictures of Mr. Lewis. Or we bring the petition onstage and read it or something."

"Could work," says Quag. "Could work."

Everyone at the lunch table turns and stares at Quagmire. Even Lily and Nick, the polite kids. They stare at him, sitting there with his orange-stained thumbs. Jake's aware that his mouth is actually open, and he doesn't even bother to shut it. This is a first. No one has ever heard anything remotely positive come out of Quag's mouth. Ever.

It is as surprising to hear Quag say "Could work" as it would be to have a little old lady in an embroidered cardigan stop Jake in the hall at church and say, "We're going to go hot-wire the pastor's car and take a joyride, kid. Then we gotta rob the bank. Let's go."

Except this is backwards. Instead of the church lady turning evil, Quag is turning good. Or something. Jake doesn't even know. It's incredibly confusing.

"It could," Quag insists. "But it would need a few things to make it *really* work."

The bell rings. Kids around them get up, start off to class. But it takes everyone at their lunch table a full ten seconds to stop staring at Quagmire Tiarello and begin gathering their stuff up.

What just happened?

CASSIE

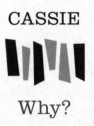

Why?

CASSIE SHOULDERS THROUGH the crowd in the hallway after last bell. All roiling bodies and sound. Slammed lockers. Backpack zippers. Shrieks from Mira Gainsley, wanting attention, always, always, from whoever happens to be near her. Snatches of conversation that change as Cassie changes hallways. Near the locker rooms, verbal chest-thumping about the basketball game tonight. Jayda Bennett and Hector Melendez arguing about something to do with wormholes as Cassie turns into the science corridor. Navya and Max discussing a scene in the spring play as Cassie rounds the corner into the drama hallway. "I mean, I'm not exactly sure how he wants me to die. Do I *die* die, or am I fatally wounded but not dead yet?"

Cassie clanks open the impossibly heavy door to the sound booth. It whooshes shut behind her. Leaves her in silence and darkness.

She feels her way up the stairs. Pulls open the last door. Quagmire's sitting in the dark, the green lights from the soundboard reflecting onto the sharp bones of his face.

"Hey," she says, sliding the lights up a little.

"'Sup?"

"What did you mean at the lunch table today?" Cassie asks.

He raises an eyebrow at her.

"What did you mean?" she asks again. "You said Mac's protest thing could work. But it needs a few tweaks?" Then, before he can answer, she asks what she really needs to know: "Why do you even care about Jazz Lab?"

Quag checks his headphones with his thumb to make sure his microphone's off. Then doesn't say a word. Just looks at her. He looks her in the eye, nothing shifty, not avoiding, just straight at her with those strange, supernova eyes.

Cassie looks back. Looking for the joke. Looking for the angle. Looking for the lie.

Then, still looking at her, he shrugs. Just shoulders up and down, once.

"Tell me what changes would make the protest work," she says.

And he does.

CASSIE

Boxes

ON THE WAY HOME FROM SCHOOL, the gray sky that's been hovering all day gets serious. Starts to rain. Cassie doesn't even care. She's thinking about Quag. About the plan they just came up with. Take over the spring concert. Make people listen to them. She's admitting to herself that Quagmire Tiarello is a surprising person.

No. "Surprising" isn't good enough. Quagmire Tiarello is a little mind-blowing. Seemed like just this kid with a majorly bad attitude. Then you start to notice. The way he sits. The way he looks at someone. What he says when he bothers to say something. He's just saying what everybody else is thinking. He's brave enough to call it out. To be right out there and let everybody know what he thinks, whether they like it or not. Cassie wishes she had the guts to do that.

She thought she had everyone in the middle school pegged by now. Guess not. Didn't see him coming. Wrote him off like he was nothing.

Whatever Quagmire Tiarello is, he's not anything like nothing.

She strolls along Elizabeth Street. Tilts her head up to feel the rain fall gently on her face. The rain quickens as she turns onto Thatcher. Then comes down like someone pulled the plug on a giant bath. A really cold, giant bath.

Cassie runs. By the time she gets home, there's a jacket-shaped dry strip around her top, but everything else is soaked through. She's freezing. Ditches her shoes and socks at the door. Squelches her way back to her room to change.

Hands wet and shaking, she can't turn the doorknob on her bedroom door. Finally twists her T-shirt around it to get a grip. Throws her shoulder against the door and stumbles into her room. It hasn't been redecorated since the first time she lived here, when she was going through her regrettable all-pink phase. The dorky pink shag rug feels great on her bare, wet feet though. She closes her eyes. Snuggles her toes into it. She is so cold. She needs cocoa. A huge vat of it. Big enough to swim in.

She doesn't notice the boxes at first.

She doesn't notice because she's shivering over to her dresser. Digging for a hoodie. Looking for her llama socks. She doesn't notice because the boxes aren't made up into boxes yet. They're brand-new, flat, fold-them-yourself boxes. The kind you buy from U-Haul. Stacked on her bed with a shiny new roll of packing tape. She doesn't notice until she goes to sit down on the edge of her bed to change. Then there they are.

Moving boxes.

The fat, cheerful, pink-and-yellow flowers marching across the wallpaper in front of her waver. The cold in her fingers and toes shoots deep into her center.

No.

No.

He said they were staying here. That Cece would move in with them here. He promised.

She can hear her dad thunking around in his room. She's down the hall in three seconds and has his door open. For an instant she sees that he knows exactly what she's upset about and wishes that he'd managed not to be here when she found those boxes. But he wipes the apprehension off his face and goes with a big smile and a "Fall in a pool on your way home?" He bites off the strip of tape he's unrolled and tapes up the box sitting on his dresser.

"You said we were staying here."

"Nah, I'm sick of this dump. Buddy of mine's starting a job in New Orleans a few weeks from now. Putting in a big development. You'll love it there. Great food, great music down there."

"Dad, you're getting married tomorrow."

"Wedding's off. Broke up this morning. Getting too

complicated." He takes a stack of T-shirts out of a drawer. "Guess you're pretty happy about that, huh? You never liked her anyway."

Cassie feels cold. Colder than rain could make her. And like something inside is peeling away from her bones. "You broke up this morning?"

He frowns and starts taping up a new box. "That's what I said. You got a problem with that?"

"You said we'd stay here though."

"Gotta go where the money is, Cass. Fact of life. Never gonna make it big in a little town like this."

She knows she shouldn't say it. She knows he'll hate her for saying it. She says it.

"You promised."

His jaw tightens.

"You promised we'd stay!" She's louder than she meant to be.

He tumbles a bunch of socks into the box.

"No!" she says. "I'm not going. Everyone's here! Everyone I care about is here! I won't go!"

He leans back against the dresser, arms crossed over his chest, eyes unfriendly. "You're not eighteen, Cassie. You can't really do no." He pushes past her and slams out the front door. She hears his truck start up. Hears him drive off fast. And she's sinking down against the faded wallpaper in the hall, arms over her head, hot tears streaking her cold cheeks.

When she was in third grade, she used to brag about her dad to Lily all the time. Back then, Cassie thought he was as cool as he thought he was. But one day, Lily came to Cassie's house, and Cassie's dad did his whole coolest-dad-in-the-universe routine. Lily stood and watched him go through his paces. And somehow as Cassie watched her watch him, Cassie understood that something was off.

Lily didn't say anything. But after that day, they always played at Lily's house instead of Cassie's. Lily didn't make a big deal out of it. It just happened that way. Without either of them ever talking about why.

Years later, after the second move back, when Cassie was telling Lily something her dad had promised her, Lily looked at her and said, "Cassie, your dad lies." Like it was a fact that everybody knew, and she was reminding Cassie because she'd forgotten. Like Lily would have said, "The math worksheet is due on Wednesday." Or "We have a half day next Friday, remember?" Or "Cassie, your dad lies."

And Cassie knew it was true.

So how does she keep forgetting?

JAKE

Only Thing Worse

SO NOW JAKE KNOWS that the only thing worse than having an aunt at his house getting ready for her wedding tomorrow and an enormous bouquet taking up his refrigerator and the entire place smelling like hair spray is to have his aunt in his living room, mascara and tears running down her face because she isn't getting married tomorrow after all. It's probably just as well and everything, but even though she made him wear hideous roses on his ankles, and even though he gets tired of this whole wedding obsession, she's still his Aunt Cece—his aunt who tells dumb knock-knock jokes and just wants life to be fun. He hates to see her so sad, like she really thought this time it would work.

It'll be better for Cassie, too, probably. Though Jake was starting to get used to the idea of being cousins with her. Cassie's okay.

LILY

On the Dock

LILY HAS STOOD ON THIS DOCK a thousand, thousand times—every sunny summer day since she was three. She has felt the weathered boards rough under her bare feet. And what she always loved, why she always came here, was the *flup, flup* of the little waves curling under the dock, hitting the pilings, rolling their collection of pebbles against the shore. Even when a big wave, churned up by some faraway boat, splashed cold drops up through the slats, the lake would quiet the splashing and smooth the lurching of the dock as soon as it could.

It always wanted peace.

So did Lily.

But now she is standing out here while the wind whips her hair and the water heaves itself at the dock again and again, waves breaking and breaking—regathering every time to hurl itself at the slippery boards.

And that seems right today.

Lily waited all morning to talk to her dad, sitting on the

stairs outside her parents' bedroom so she wouldn't miss him, taking his smile as he came down as a good sign. And she told him about what Cassie texted her last night. About how Cassie's dad was going to move her again and how Lily had figured out that Cassie could move in with them so she wouldn't have to leave. She told him how Cassie could share her room. She told him how she didn't want Cassie to go away again.

And all he said was "Out of the question."

When Lily asked why and told him only till the end of the school year and then, finally, desperate, said Cassie could help her with her math and biology grades, he looked at her, blew on his coffee, and said, "You spend too much time with Cassie. And that jazz band thing. You've had your fun with that, but the time investment may not be worth it in light of your grades. Next year, I want you back in orchestra where you belong. More structure." Then he went into his office and closed the door so he wouldn't even have to pretend to listen to her.

The water hisses under the boards of the dock, and the surface of the lake heaves, gray and white and dangerous. Looking at it right now, Lily can't help but think that it might smash and shatter and destroy.

Peace is the last thing on its mind.

MAC

Rules

DON'T TALK BACK TO TEACHERS.

Cooperate.

Help people get along. Smooth out problems.

Work hard.

Be someone people can count on.

Do the right thing.

Do the right thing.

Do the right thing.

But what if the thing that feels like the right thing means you'll break a lot of those other rules?

CASSIE

All In

"HEY, MAC." CASSIE SLIDES her saxophone case under the lunch table and sits down. "Think you can get some representatives from each of the electives and clubs to come over here real quick?"

The news about the petition ending up in the trash has been all over the school the last couple of days, and Cassie's talked to she-doesn't-know-how-many people who found her in the halls or in the locker room or at her desk before class about that and about the school board meeting, but now it's time to get organized about this protest.

"Sure," says Mac. "All of them? Turns out there's a lot of them."

"All of them," says Cassie. "To make this thing work, we need everybody."

QUAGMIRE

Borrowing

QUAGMIRE CAN TELL that Mr. Saavedra is surprised to see him when he stops by his weird closet office after play practice on Monday. But Quag asks him a couple of questions that are legit-sounding and technical enough to be impressive. While Mr. Saavedra logs in to his computer to pull up the spec sheets for the soundboard, Quag eyes the keys on his desk.

He knows the two he needs. He could probably snake the whole keychain off the desk, but among the sixty-seven or so keys on that ring, Quag can see a Volkswagen key. So Saavedra would notice his keys were missing as soon as he hit the parking lot, if not sooner.

So, now what?

He could prop the doors open, but all it would take was a careful janitor, and the whole plan would go up in flames.

But then there are peals of laughter from the hall and some serious slamming into lockers, and Quag has never been quite so glad for the general idiocy of Brandt Felton and Grady Magdill and their timely decision to simulate a pinball game in the hall with a couple of derelict roller chairs that have been sitting in a pile waiting for repairs. Because while Mr. Saavedra is out in the hall, repossessing the chairs and sending Brandt and Grady on their way, the two keys Quag needs disappear into his pocket, and three cables from the pegboard disappear into his backpack.

JAKE

Getting Ready

"BIGGER THAN THAT," SAYS QUAG.

"It's a queen sheet," says Mac. "Where we gonna get something bigger than that?"

Coach Brody, who's on lunch monitor duty today, is clearly wondering why Mac has half a floral sheet pulled out of his backpack. Jake nudges Mac with an elbow, and he stuffs it back in the pack.

"That won't look like anything up on the stage," says Quag. "We've got to have something really big."

"A tarp?" asks Nick. "We got a pretty big tarp over our woodpile. It might have a couple of holes in it though. And it's kind of puke green."

"What about a canvas drop cloth?" asks Cassie. "My dad has a huge canvas drop cloth in his truck for jobs. One that covers a whole room."

"Yes," says Quag. "Get the drop cloth."

"He won't let me use it if I ask." Cassie crosses her arms

over her chest and scowls. "I'll have to figure out how to get it out of the truck without getting caught."

"But what do we paint on it?" Mac asks. "'We heart Jazz Lab'?"

"No," says Cassie. "Sounds like a T-shirt, not a protest. And whatever we put on it has to include everyone, not just Jazz Lab." She's looking even more ferocious than usual today.

Lily pulls out a spiral notebook. "Maybe we make a list of what we want changed. You know, the things we're protesting." She starts to number the lines on the paper—*1, 2, 3*—but Cassie grabs the notebook and pulls it across the table and then motions for the pen. She holds Lily's red pen in her fist like she's going to stab something with it, then slashes it down on the paper so that she's more carving the words than writing them. *YOU DON'T LISTEN TO US!* she gouges in tall letters that cover the entire page. She throws the pen down on the tabletop.

They all look at the slanted, angry letters, torn through the paper in places. Lily traces over them with a finger.

"Yep," says Mac. "That would be it."

CASSIE

Getting Ready

THEY PRACTICE LIKE MAD in Jazz Lab. Even without Mr. Lewis. Playing again. Not the pathetic, trying-to-play stuff they've been doing since Mr. Lewis left. The real deal. Mac slamming then whispering across the keys. Lily playing with that look on her face that lets you know she's gotten to that place where music just pours out of her fingertips. Even the sub with the phone addiction takes notice, index finger paused to swipe left and mouth half-open as they jam.

Because they've got a plan. The school board always shows up at the spring concert, because they have this big thing where they announce the state music awards. And the school board loves anything that comes with a ribbon. So Jazz Lab has to be good for their plan to work. In two more days, they've got to be ready to make a statement in front of everyone at the concert.

Cassie's checked in with Ms. Harken, who always prints up the programs, to make sure Jazz Lab is still on the schedule and still playing last. And they told the sub that they always play without a conductor, that it's a tradition, and he bought that.

Mac is convinced the guy doesn't even know how to conduct, so that's why he agreed so quick. Who knows?

Playing for real again feels good. Like they're ready. Ready to make people listen.

But whenever Cassie's not in Jazz Lab, she feels like there's nothing but empty inside her. Her dad's still packing. She's got a couple of weeks if he doesn't decide to suddenly move it up. Which he could do. Everything she sees, every person she walks down the hall with, is something she's going to lose.

QUAGMIRE

Getting Ready

IF ANYONE HAD CHECKED QUAG'S backpack on Wednesday, they would have found one sleeve of bagels, a jar of peanut butter, a box of raspberry Pop-Tarts, a flashlight, a sleeping bag, his mom's laptop, and two keys Quag had stolen from Mr. Saavedra's desk.

No one checks. Teachers have long since given up on Quagmire getting textbooks and assignments out of that backpack on any regular basis. He does enough stuff to pass his classes, but just barely.

Today, Quag actually turns in homework that's due, doesn't argue with anyone in the classrooms or halls, and manages to avoid seeing Mr. Deming all day long. Then he checks out of ninth period with a pass and says he has to set up sound equipment for a performance.

And he does go straight to the auditorium. He takes care of the mikes that Mr. Saavedra has left for him to set up. But he doesn't go back to class. He carefully opens the trapdoor in the floor of the stage and goes down to the weird little storage room underneath where Mr. Saavedra had sent some of the kids on crew once to look for another lamp after Brendon tripped over the one they'd had on set and demolished it. Quag goes past the stored profiles and Fresnels, through a forest of decrepit mike stands and dead AV equipment, and around an old set involving some kind of barn. Way in the back, he pushes stuff to the side until he clears a space by an old plaid stage couch. He rolls out his sleeping bag on the couch, texts his mom to tell her he's staying at a friend's house overnight and will be going to school from there, and sets an alarm for 9:00 p.m. Then he eats three raspberry Pop-Tarts and goes to sleep.

The silence wakes him before his alarm rings. Even down in the little room under the stage, Quag can feel the silence. No voices, no footsteps, no bells, no markers on whiteboards, no rustling paper—all that lack of sound is what he climbs up into when he carefully opens the trapdoor and comes out.

The school feels weird. So much empty in a space that was made to be full. He sits in the dark with only the pale green of the exit sign falling over him and listens. He can hear his own breathing, and when a blower turns on with a sigh, he feels like the building is breathing back at him, waiting to see what he'll do.

What he does is eat two peanut butter bagels and wait for

one more hour, because he figures not even a janitor will still be working after ten at night. Then he climbs up to the sound booth, turns on the lights, googles some stuff on the laptop, and, floating there in a gleaming bubble suspended above the auditorium, he gets to work.

NICK

Getting Ready

"NICK?"

Nick's mom stands at his bedroom door wearing her striped green bathrobe with the ripped pocket and those polar bear slippers Nick bought for her when he was ten or something.

Nick lowers his trumpet.

"Honey, it's past midnight."

"Oh," he says. "Sorry."

"Get some sleep, okay? You've got school tomorrow. Your dad and I have work tomorrow."

"Okay."

She runs her hand through her hair. "Nick, you alright?" she asks.

"Yeah," says Nick. "I'm okay."

She looks like she's thinking of saying something else but then heads back down the hall, slippers scuffing.

Nick settles the trumpet into its case and sits on the edge of the bed. He doesn't tell her that even if he goes to sleep, he's going to wake up with his fingers running through the valve combinations for tomorrow night's concert, even though the trumpet isn't in his hand.

He doesn't tell her how he'll feel standing in the crowded backstage, waiting to play. How it's like fighting through a labyrinth as he tries to get to the stage—veer around the stacked chairs, slide around a prop room box, avoid a rack of duck costumes, dodge the stream of kids coming off from the number before—how his gut will twist tighter and tighter as he gets closer, because he knows, he knows, that as soon as he slips through that last layer of curtains, he will be standing there in a spotlight like he's under an interrogation lamp and the whole middle school has gathered to watch the shakedown.

He doesn't tell her that even with all that, he's going to do it, and that he wants to do it well, because he's afraid, he's so afraid, that this might be the last time he and his friends will get to play together.

MAC

Getting Ready

MAC KNOCKS ON MARI'S BEDROOM DOOR as soon as he hears Mom's car pull out of the driveway.

"Yeah?" she yells.

He opens the door and sticks his head through. Mari's sitting at her desk with three books spread across it—all the books, SLAM BLAM, full of Post-its. She's in serious study mode. "Can I come in?" Mac asks.

"Because . . . ?" She's got her eyebrows raised in warning. "Important? Or just to hang out? This paper is due tomorrow."

"Important."

She sweeps a pile of note cards off the beanbag chair next to her desk. "Sit. Short and sweet version. What's up?"

"You know your friend that plays jazz flute?"

"Jaron, yeah. What about it?"

"Is he in your high school? Is he in Jazz Ensemble?"

"No, he goes to West. I thought you said this was important." She's already back to scribbling notes.

Mac takes a big breath. "Mari, you know how you're supposed to do what's right no matter what?"

"Yeaaaaaah." She's looking at him now and has moved to a one-eyebrow-up, one-eyebrow-down configuration. It's even more forbidding.

"But you know how you're also supposed to cooperate with people and talk things out and be good and not get in trouble?"

"Yep."

"What if you can't do both?"

"Mac, did you do something stupid?"

"How come you always think I've done something stupid?"

"You're the kid who ate glue sticks."

"Once, Mari. Once. And I was four. Also, it smelled like grape popsicles."

"Yeah. Point carried. So I have to ask. Have you, or have you not, done something really stupid?"

"I haven't. Thanks for the vote of confidence. I don't even know why I bothered to come talk to you." Mac rolls out of the beanbag and turns for the door.

"Sorry," Mari says, grabbing his arm. "Sit down." She closes the US history book in front of her and spins around in her chair. "Talk to me, Mac."

Mac sinks back down and fiddles with the zipper on the beanbag. What is he allowed to tell her? Like what if she thinks the whole thing is stupid? Just adds it to the boy-who-ate-purple-glue list? What if she decides to tell Mom and Dad?

She's still giving him her eyebrow-workout look. "So," she says, "you have not done anything stupid, but you are thinking of doing something stupid, or at least something that Mom, Dad, teachers, other authority figures won't like?"

"Basically."

"But you think it's right."

"Yeah."

"How much trouble are you going to get in?"

"Don't know. Could be a lot."

"Are you breaking any laws?"

"No."

"Hurting anybody?"

"No."

"But you're going to piss some people off."

"Probably."

"Because you're going to be a jerk about it? Or because someone won't like what you have to say?"

"Second one."

"Huh." She's tapping her pen on her pack of Post-its and staring at the wall. "Is it about something important to you, or something that won't matter in two years?"

"WAY SUPER important."

She swings back around and gives him a long look, then sighs. "Might have to do it, then."

"That's what I thought too." Mac leans back into the bean-bag chair. ZIP, ZAP. He feels better now. He feels like stealing that pen and pencil right off Mari's desk and beating out a little MAC ATTACK joy riff on her books. Which would probably get him killed. "Want to know what we're doing?" he asks her.

"Uh-uh," Mari says. "Do *not* tell me. More I know, more spillover trouble I catch. I don't know a thing. Deal?"

"Deal." He stands and heads toward her door.

"Mac," she says as he reaches for the knob.

"What?"

"Just don't be stupid, okay?"

LILY

Getting Ready

LILY'S DAD LIKES THE CLASSICAL STUFF she used to play in orchestra, but he doesn't like the music she plays in Jazz Lab. He says it sounds messy. So she usually practices when he's not home.

But tonight she doesn't care. She gets out her bow, which she's hardly used this year, and slashes it across the strings until it slides off with a screech. And then she does it again. Again. Again. Again. Until it sounds like her bass is moaning and crying in pain. The bass shivers, and the bow crashes, crashes, crashes, and her cheek is crushed against the hard wood of the neck, and her fingers mash the strings into the fingerboard over and over.

The door to the room swings open, and her dad's voice sweeps in behind her. "Honestly, Lily. Are you *trying* to play something ugly? I can't even hear myself think."

Silence falls. She hears the door close again. Her breath is ragged and loud in the quiet room.

Yes, Dad. I am trying to play something ugly.

MAC

Concert Tomorrow

HERE'S HOW MAC FEELS ABOUT CONCERTS:

Like someone handed him a big old present in bright red paper with a swirly gold bow, and he just knows that whatever is in that box is something he wants, something he has always wanted.

Like he's been given permission to dance down the halls between classes and that everybody in those sad, gray corridors will spill out of the classrooms and dance along with him, just like in a musical.

Like someone walked up behind him and lowered a crown onto his head, and for those few awesome moments onstage, he is the king of some world that runs on sound and rhythm and joy. And he'll tip that crown back at an angle, because a king should always wear a crown lightly, and lift his hands over the keys of his piano and set that world spinning.

LILY

Safety

LILY HAS ALWAYS LOVED SAFETY. When she was little and all the other kids screamed with joy and ran straight to the slides and the monkey bars, she stayed holding on to her mom's leg, watching. After a while, she would go on the swings, but a swing is tethered. You fly out in an arc and come back, out and back, out and back, always back, always feeling that solid thump of your mom's next push, her touch launching every flight and welcoming you back again.

That's what Lily loves. Safety. But she doesn't feel safe anymore. She feels like she has something to say that is too important to be ignored, but that she can ask, or cry, or beg, or plead, and people will still brush past her like she's making no sound at all. Maybe that's why she sits down in that chair and says, "Do it," when Nick comes in with those hair clippers.

CASSIE

Clippers

WHEN NICK COMES into the practice room where Cassie and the other kids are warming up for the concert and pulls out these electric hair clippers and says, "We should shave our heads. Like the soccer players did when they went to State. Like a team unity thing to protest them shaving Jazz Lab out of the budget. Get it?" everyone just laughs.

Except Nick, who stands there holding those shiny black clippers, and Cassie can see that he wasn't joking at all.

And except Lily.

Lily gets this strange, intense, completely not-the-usual-Lily look on her face. She plunks herself down in the chair and says, "Do it."

They're all so surprised, it's like an instant shot of serious to the whole room. Because Lily means it. Everyone gathers around the chair. "Lily, are you sure?" Cassie asks. Lily nods twice. Grabs the clippers out of Nick's hand. Gives them to Cassie.

She gives them to Cassie, who takes them but then freezes, staring at Lily's hair. Lily has the most beautiful hair. Beautiful.

When you first see it, you think "black." Because it is — black and shiny and down to the middle of her back. But if you really look at it, it's black with streaks of deep brown. Even something leaning toward red.

Lily doesn't care that it's gorgeous. Usually just has it looped up in a ponytail or hanging loose. But Cassie loves Lily's hair. Cassie used to sit and braid it for hours when they were little. Sometimes when Cassie's upset, she still does. It still helps. So she stands there with those clippers in her hand, and she feels like she's about to slash a Van Gogh in a museum. Seems wrong.

But Lily's not joking. Lily doesn't let people see that part of her too often, but she's fierce. She's just fierce in a quiet, need-to-know kind of way.

"Do it," Lily says again.

The button on the side of the clippers is black and grooved and hard to slide. Leaves a tiny three-lined mark on Cassie's thumb as she clicks it over. The clippers purr to life. She pulls a long strand of hair up from Lily's forehead.

She starts cutting.

Jake is standing behind Lily's chair. His eyes are huge, like an extremely disturbed frog's. He makes a quiet sound in his throat and turns his back on them like he can't watch.

Lily closes her eyes. One tear runs down the right side of

her face. Cassie's cutting. Lily's hair is falling. Onto Lily's shirt. Her lap. The floor.

Cassie's hands are shaking so bad she's afraid she'll cut Lily. At a certain point, Cassie realizes her face is wet and that she's crying so hard tears are dripping off her chin. Mac comes to stand by her, and slowly, like she's something dangerous, he reaches over, gently takes the clippers from her, and finishes cutting Lily's hair while Nick pats Cassie on the back like some sort of kindly, awkward human metronome.

Then Mac shaves Cassie's hair. And Nick's hair. And Jake's hair.

There's a moment halfway through Jake's shave when the clippers seize up, and they think Jake's going to have to go onstage one-third bald and two-thirds floppy brown, and everyone gets the giggles. Everyone except Jake, who looks more panicked than Cassie's ever seen him.

Nick gets this tube of oil and a tiny brush out of the clipper bag. Messes around with the clippers till he gets them going again and finishes off Jake's hair. And Mac's.

There's a blanket of sleek black, wavy brown, straight ashy brown, curly ginger, and wiry black all over the floor and five bald, big-eyed kids standing in a circle, staring at each other, when Mr. Conroy sticks his head into the room. He starts to say, "Five minutes," which is his usual way of telling them to get themselves ready to go. Then he sees them. Says something Cassie's pretty sure teachers aren't supposed to say inside the school.

But they all pick up their instruments and walk past poor, open-mouthed Mr. Conroy and out toward the stage. And Cassie's proud of them. Because they all walk like they know what they're doing.

JAKE

What They Do

THERE'S A COMPLETE TRAFFIC JAM in the wings of the stage because concert band is coming off as Jazz Lab's coming on, and when the first concert band kids see them — five kids with heads bare under the stage lights — they stop cold and stare, and the kids behind them crash into them, and the kids behind them want to know what the heck. It's a mess. Jake goes around the whole pileup and heads to the far side of the stage with his clarinet in hand while they get themselves sorted out.

The auditorium is packed. The seats are full and there are people standing in the back. And a lot of the people in the room are kids from their school. Just like they planned.

A whisper washes through the crowd as Jazz Lab walks across the stage and takes their seats.

And then the lights go out.

Jake sits there with his clarinet in the dark, his scalp feeling raw and weirdly cold, and waits. He hears the others settling into their chairs. Quag keeps the lights off long enough that people are getting nervous. Somehow, he's even managed to turn off all the exit signs, which, okay, that's illegal, but it's Quag. So the blackness is thick, inky. The whispers from the audience start up again. And Jake remembers that Quag told him this would happen. That Quag said, "Wait long enough. Wait till you have their attention. Wait till just before they start to panic."

So Jake waits. The whispers eddy around and then start to build and swirl up onto the stage and up into the rafters. And then, when even Jake may be starting to panic, he gathers every angry thought, everything he's felt about losing the thing that is most important to him, about no one thinking that what he wants is important, about no one listening to him, and he lets his clarinet cry like it is the beginning and end of all sorrows. He sends that cry out into the blackness, and there is the silence of five hundred people who've forgotten how to breathe in the auditorium. And he just lets his music sing to them about everything they've ever hoped for and lost, and then Cassie brings in one of those saxophone wails that she loves to do, and when everyone's hearts are about to split in unison, they all roll out the jazz fast and hot and sweet. Quag brings the lights up on them, and then he is somehow flashing images on the walls all over the auditorium, and some are photos of people with signs and people marching, and some are pictures of signs that Cassie and Quag painted, and even more are pictures Cassie took of the kids in the electives and clubs that might be getting cut—Cory with his hands full of curly lettuce leaves, and Sam using some kind of hand tool that makes long shavings, and Dev and Aisha and Tipton and Saima—and they're huge and beautiful and the whole effect is pretty freaking epic. Their banner comes rippling down: LISTEN UP! WE WANT A VOICE IN WHAT WE LEARN! Mac's going nuts on the piano and Nick is sending a string of bright notes out over the crowd and Lily is playing with her eyes closed. Jake loves it when Lily plays with her eyes closed.

And when Mac hits some massive chords and then raises his arms and all the kids from the school leap to their feet and start chanting, "LISTEN UP! LISTEN UP! LISTEN UP! LISTEN UP!" as Mac conducts them between the chords, Jake remembers back to fourth grade and that jazz quartet in Syracuse that his mom took him to see. The dark auditorium. How they played. And Jake wonders if they felt this way, like somehow something in their chests was opening like a time-lapse flower.

Because tonight, Jazz Lab is that good. Jake will never forget this. They controlled this audience. They told them when to breathe.

And the audience listened.

NICK

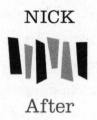

After

NICK HADN'T THOUGHT about what would happen afterward. The furthest he'd let himself think was how his breath would wind through the leadpipe, how his fingers would pump the valve pistons.

He hadn't imagined this.

Wow.

Wow. Wow. Wow.

People are going wild.

Wow. They're still clapping.

When the lights had gone out, Nick had sat, his hands cold, the stiff plastic of the chair pressing against his back and legs, and when the cry from Jake's clarinet went out into the dark, it felt like it pulled on something in Nick's chest that made it hard for him to breathe. And he looked out and thought, *Why not? Why not? It's the last time we'll ever play together. Why not?*

So he closed his eyes and imagined that he belonged. That he belonged, and the people out in the dark had come all the way to a little club in New York City, and they'd all come to hear him, Nick Finlay. And when the music curled around him and he felt a spot where the bright notes from a trumpet would make a sweet and shining thing, he played like the band would follow him. And they did follow him.

And then how they played. How they all played.

Wow.

He looks out at the crowd of people, some on their feet, yelling and whistling, some sitting, stunned, and he's searching for two people. He knows where they'll be, his dad in the clean plaid shirt he wears when he's dressing up, his mom, scrubbed and wearing her green sweater, both way over to the left like they're trying not to take up too much space, trying not to be seen.

Except they're not sitting. They're standing. His mom is wiping at tears. And when Nick catches his dad's eyes, his dad gives him one slow nod. And the tears and the nod mean as much to Nick as anything that's happened tonight. They do.

MAC

After

MAC'S DANCING BEHIND THE PIANO to the music of applause and shouts and whistles and—SLAMA JAMA BAM!—he feels GOOD!

Once Mr. Conroy, sweating and red-faced, calms everyone down and thanks the audience for coming and quickly ends the concert, Mari runs up the stage steps to give Mac a big hug.

"Nice!" she says. "That was so much more impressive than glue eating. Nice," she says again, folding him up in another hug. Then she stands back and gives him a serious look. "Okay, just so you know, our parents are majorly freaked out by all this. But also a little awed. Could go either way. So the way we play it is that this was an act of conscience, got it?"

"Got it," says Mac, and he's glad Mari's on his side, but he also does not CARE if they get into twelve FLAVORS of trouble over this. Totally, TOTALLY AWESOME! "WOOOOOOOOOOOOOOO!!!!!!"

QUAGMIRE

After

QUAGMIRE CLICKS THE BOARD OFF, removes his headphones, and leans back in the creaky chair.

Sweet.

He wishes Cassie were up here. Wishes he could look across at her and see her trying not to smile in that way that means she's ultra-pleased with what happened but doesn't want to go all mushy about it.

But he can see her from up here. Standing on the stage, holding the saxophone over her head like it's the Stanley Cup or something. Like some sort of warrior. Bald. When did that happen? Wearing a black T-shirt that says ALL I WANT IS ALL THAT JAZZ.

The crowd's finally settling down. The members of Jazz Lab head off the stage. Through a gap in the curtains, he can see backstage and the big hug fest and high-five-a-thon that has broken out there. Somehow, watching it makes Quag feel like a little hole that shouldn't be there is opening right behind his sternum, and it hurts, and since no one's there to see, he rubs his fist hard across it, but it doesn't help. Maybe feels like it's getting even bigger, so he has to stop watching the band kids and start coiling up the cables. When he looks again, they're gone.

He puts away the laptop and clicks all the switches back to their off positions. He bets no one in this school has ever used as many switches as he did tonight. He runs his fingers over the board and shuts it down. He peels off the sound tape he used for the show and wads it up.

There's a knock on the door.

Cassie.

For a split second, he thinks about stealing her chair before she opens the door, but then he grins and drops into the creaky chair, leaning back and crossing his arms over his chest. But the knob just rattles.

Oh, yeah. He locked it. And he has the key.

He rolls in his chair across the booth and swings the door open.

Oh.

Not Cassie.

Mr. Saavedra.

Mr. Saavedra looking tense and grim and royally pissed off. Saavedra holds his hand out, palm up. "Keys," he says.

Quagmire could deny it. Saavedra won't pat him down, he

knows it. Might take him to Deming, but Quag could ditch the keys somewhere during one of those lapses of attention teachers have when they're super angry and talking to each other about what to do to you. But for some reason, Quag digs in his pocket and drops the keys—one wrapped in green iguana tape, one in orange electrical tape—into Saavedra's hand.

Mr. Saavedra looks at them a long time, like keys are things that might get up and dance on his palm or something. Then, finally, he closes his fist over them and sighs, his face relaxing into lines of weariness. "You're off the crew, Quagmire," he says. "You're done." He motions for the cables on the desk. Quag hands them over and moves toward the door.

Saavedra blocks his way. "Not because of this." He gestures out toward the auditorium. "I have never seen lights and sound handled like that. That was the most amazing work, bar none, that I have ever seen from a middle school kid." He turns and looks out at the auditorium as if he can still see the lights and the pictures flashing across the walls, then shakes his head.

"You're out because of the trust thing. I have to be able to trust you."

CASSIE

After

LIGHT SPILLS OUT THE STEEL DOOR behind the stage, and Cassie sees that someone's jammed a folded magazine under the door to keep it open. Outside, beyond the thin rectangle of light thrown by the door, it's dark. And cold. A couple of dumpsters loom up to her left. "Quag?" she yells out into the night.

Nothing. He's not in the sound booth. It's locked, empty. And now he's not here? Where is he?

She steps into the darkness. A cold wind stirs some trash at the base of the dumpsters.

"Quag?" she tries again.

She feels rather than hears someone behind her. And there he is, leaning against the brick wall in the shadow behind the door, silent.

"Why didn't you answer me?" Cassie asks. But he doesn't answer her.

He stands there.

He stands there, like he always stands there, like she's seen him stand there three thousand times in all the years since third grade. Stands there, like they haven't just done the most amazing thing either of them has ever done in their lives. Stands there, eyes looking slightly to the left of her. Like they aren't even friends. Like she's Mr. Deming. Or Ms. Morales. Or an empty plastic bag blowing around in front of the dumpster.

A wild sorrow wells up in her heart.

It wasn't real. All of this wasn't real. It was just a way for him to get back at all those teachers he hates. To show everybody up again. To be smarter than everybody else. And now it's over, and he's shown them, and he's going to go back to being like he's always been. Everybody shut out. Her, shut out.

And she hates him for it. She wants to scream at him. Wants to reach out and put both palms against his chest and smash him into the wall. Wants to throw a right hook and shatter his nose.

But she is going to leave without doing any of those things. Because she can feel the tight ache in her throat and the burning along her eyelids, and she is not going to cry in front of him.

A movement in the shadow. And now she's watching him raise his hand from his side, and all she can think is that he has bigger hands than she ever realized. Such long fingers. And those fingers brush gently along her jaw, back to her ear, up to where the stubble starts.

"You shaved your head," he says.

"Yeah," she says.

"Cool."

LILY

After

AFTER IT'S OVER, LILY GOES DOWN and finds her family. Her mom puts her hand over her mouth and makes this funny half-laugh, half-sob noise, and her eyes look like she might move all the way to the sobbing side any second, but she pulls Lily into a hug and then holds her at arm's length and turns her from side to side, looking at her head, and says, "Well, that's going to take a while to grow out," and cry-laughs a little more.

Lily's nonna takes her hand and says, "Okay, then. We should talk about this when we get home. Still, I liked your music tonight, my Lily."

But Lily's dad won't even look at her. Or walk with them. He goes straight out to the car. And when they get there, he does not say one word all the way home.

JAKE

After

WHEN JAKE FINALLY FINDS HIS MOM afterward, she is sitting in the almost empty auditorium, waiting for him. "Did not expect that," she says.

"Pretty epic, huh?"

"Um, yes. Though not everyone may see it quite that way." She sighs and holds her phone out to him. A text from Aunt Terri is open on the screen: "Seriously, Audrey? Again? Is he TRYING to make me look bad? We need to talk."

"How come she wants to talk to you?" says Jake. "You didn't have anything to do with this."

His mom shrugs.

"She doesn't think kids can think and do stuff on our own. We can."

"Obviously," says his mom. She clicks over to an email and shows Jake the phone again. "Please call at your earliest convenience to schedule a meeting between your student, yourself, and Principal Deming concerning this evening's insubordinate behavior at the concert."

Great.

Mom folds down the seat next to her, and Jake sinks into it. "Um, Jake. It was amazing, but I kind of wish . . ." She runs her hands through her hair and leans back in her chair. "Why didn't you talk to me about this?"

Seriously? Jake thinks it first, but this time he's too mad to not say it out loud.

"Seriously, Mom?" He can't believe she just asked him that question. "I tried to talk to you about this like three hundred seventy-four times! But you were all like, 'Sorry, can't talk to you about your favorite teacher; sorry, can't talk to you because I have to pick up the bride's bouquet; sorry, can't talk to you because I have one hundred twenty-five campaign signs to deliver; sorry, can't talk because I have to answer my phone so my sisters can yell at me. Sorry!'"

He's mad and not even trying to be nice about it, and he expects his mom to be mad right back, and he doesn't even care. But his mom's face looks more surprised than angry. She slides down in her seat and props her head against the back of the chair and looks up at the ceiling. She lets out a long sigh. "You did try. You're right. I didn't listen."

Yeah. You didn't listen.

JAKE

Next Morning

IT TOOK JAKE A LONG TIME to get to sleep after the concert last night. He kept turning everything they'd done over and over in his head. How it felt to play like that. How it felt when all those other kids joined in.

And, okay, it's caused major trouble with Deming, which you had to kind of expect, but which is still freaking Jake out. Because he's not sure how major the major trouble will be. Also, the head-shaving thing hadn't really been part of the plan; that just sort of happened, so he expects comments about the bald head at school. He spent time practicing responses this morning in the mirror. "Almost summer. Gotta go with the high-ventilation haircut, man." Stuff like that.

What he did not expect was to see a group of bald kids waiting for him right inside the school door. They give a whoop when Jake walks in. He recognizes the kids from the chess club. "Solidarity," says Cade, rubbing his shiny head. "We shaved in solidarity."

Jake works his way toward the science wing, and not one person makes fun of the haircut. In fact, there are a few people beyond just the chess kids sporting the shave this morning. Mira Gainsley and a couple of her friends are trying to get in on the whole thing by wearing bald caps, though they're letting their long hair hang out the bottom of them. Trust Mira to try to look like she's part of a movement without messing up her hair.

A big bald kid comes toward Jake, a hand up for a high five. Jake returns it, but it takes him a minute to place the face. It's Peyton! His golden-locks cousin is completely, emphatically bald.

"Looks good," says Jake, nodding toward the haircut.

For the record, it does not look good. Without the golden mane, Peyton is just a tall, lumpy-headed kid with big teeth. But Peyton looks pretty happy with it, and Jake appreciates the support.

"Told my mom I was quitting soccer," says Peyton. "She had a total screaming meltdown, but my dad backed me up. Said to let me sit out a season and then I'll know if I want it."

Seems like every single kid stops to talk to Jake as he walks down the hall.

"That was awesome!"

"My mom thought she was going to have to drag me to the concert last night because my little sister plays trombone in concert band. But then I was like, of course I'll go, and she couldn't figure out what was going on. It was so awesome when we all started chanting 'Listen up!' together."

"You were totally legit."

"Dude. I thought Deming was going to blow. When that big sign came down from the ceiling, he was like, 'What?' You should have seen his face."

"That music was seriously epic."

"You guys were intense."

It's like all these people who never paid one bit of attention to Jake can suddenly see him.

NICK

Next Morning

NICK'S GRANDAD MOVED IN when Nick was five. Grandad was old even then. Nick was scared of his big knobby knuckles and the papery skin with the spots and the veins showing through all purple-blue. He remembers wondering whether, if Grandad took off his shirt, you would be able to see his heart beating purple through the skin of his chest.

Yeah. Creepy idea.

Grandad made Nick twitchy. His way of looking at him from under those bushy eyebrows and saying, "Hey, kid" whenever Nick came into the house made him all kinds of jittery at first.

But eight years is a long time. It's a long time. And by the end, Nick wasn't scared of any of that stuff. He'd just "Hey, Pops" him back whenever Grandad "Hey, kidded" him, and Nick doesn't exactly talk about this at the lunch table at school, but he held those bony, papery hands for days at the end, just sitting there by the side of his grandad's bed, not talking about anything, because they'd already talked about it all and didn't need to anymore, and talking was hard for Grandad by then.

But Nick was still scared of one thing. He was scared that when his grandad died, a part of Nick's self would float off, trying to follow Grandad, and Nick wouldn't be Nick anymore. It sounds stupid now, but it felt like a real thing then.

In a way, it was. The whole spring and summer after Grandad died, Nick did things without knowing what he did. Like somehow he wasn't really living in his own body.

Then, one day in June, Nick was walking around the streets in town, pretty much in circles, not going anywhere, just walking so he wouldn't have to be home, where Grandad wasn't, and Mr. Lewis yelled to him from the porch of one of the houses on one of the streets he was walking along.

Nick had met Mr. Lewis before. He and Grandad were friends and would stop and talk if they met each other in the grocery store or passed each other at the park. And Nick had seen Mr. Lewis a couple of times in the halls at school.

But Nick was thinking, *What is Mr. Lewis doing at that house?* Mr. Lewis called out to Nick again, and Nick turned himself up that driveway and went over to the porch. Mr. Lewis introduced him to his wife, who was sitting there with him.

By then, Nick's brain had finally caught up and realized that this was Mr. Lewis's house, two blocks over from his own. Nick probably said something brilliant, like "Hi," but he knows that Mr. Lewis said, "Nick, I'm sorry about your grandpa," and Nick started to cry. Just standing there in the middle of the porch, bawling.

So that was super embarrassing, and Nick was trying to wipe his eyes on his T-shirt and not drop snot all over everywhere, but Mr. Lewis didn't seem to mind, and Mrs. Lewis didn't seem to mind. She said, "Sit down right here, Nicholas," and patted the flowered cushion on the porch swing, while Mr. Lewis passed him a box of tissues. And Nick just sat there and cried for a while.

Anyway, Mrs. Lewis went in and brought out some lemonade and some of those old-people cookies covered in cinnamon and sugar. And Mr. Lewis said, "I've been thinking you might try out for Jazz Lab, Nick. There's a piece I'd like you to work on. But it's a tough one. So when you have trouble with it, and you *will* have trouble with it, drop by, and we'll work on it. Because I'd like you to get this thing down well enough that you can go off-road and improvise. Okay?"

So Nick spent all the rest of the summer trying to learn this evil trumpet solo. And it was tough. Because Nick's not like Mac. He's not even like Jake. He's not a real music person. He played in band only because his mom wanted him to, and because he wasn't any good at sports.

He sure wasn't planning on trying out for Jazz Lab. He didn't even know what improvising was. He didn't know what chord progressions were. When Mr. Lewis first mentioned turnarounds, Nick thought of cars in a parking lot, not of ways of getting between sections of a song. He didn't know hardly anything.

But he got kind of obsessed with that solo. He did. He played it for hours. And he threw things. Because Lewis wasn't lying. It was killer hard. And he went down to work with Lewis on sixteenth notes and upbeats and downbeats and played it again and threw things again. But it helped to have something else to obsess over than the not-being-there of his grandad.

Once school started, Nick didn't go to Lewis's. Because Lewis seemed more like a teacher then, and going to a teacher's house would be weird. But because of last summer, Nick knows where Lewis lives.

And because of his grandad, Nick knows what a hospice nurse looks like.

So, this morning, walking to school a different way than usual so he can avoid Gabe Johnston, who lives on Nick's street and has a big mouth and will no doubt have comments about the shaved head and the concert, Nick turns onto Lewis's street. And as he comes around the corner, his whole heart goes ice-block cold, and his feet won't do anything but stand. Because that squat white truck that delivers oxygen is in Mr. Lewis's driveway, parked next to his blue Toyota, and there is a hospice nurse, with koala bears on her cheerful nurse shirt that doesn't quite hide the stethoscope hanging around her neck, standing on the porch, ringing the doorbell.

The door opens. Mrs. Lewis opens it. And then she and the nurse disappear into the house. But Nick stands, frozen on the corner.

Because now he knows. He knows.

CASSIE

Mr. Lewis

THIRTEEN MINUTES before the warning bell rang this morning, Nick sent all-caps texts to everyone in Jazz Lab saying to meet him at his locker. And when everyone except Lily, who wasn't at school, gathered there, Nick told them. How maybe they'd been wrong about what had been going on with Mr. Lewis. That he thought Mr. Lewis was sick. Really, really sick.

"We gotta go, guys," Mac said. "We gotta go see him, right now."

"We'll go during lunch," said Nick. "Nobody will miss us during lunch."

"The alarm is broken on that door between the art and tech wings," said Quag, who had been listening in. "Text me when you get back, and I'll let you in."

So they sneaked out the broken-alarm door while everybody else was headed for the lunchroom. And now Cassie, Jake, Mac, and Nick are out of school in the middle of the day, which feels super weird and a little scary, and they're walking to Mr. Lewis's house.

"This is it," says Nick. Stops in front of a pretty little gray house with a yellow door and a giant bush crammed full of hot-pink flowers by the porch. It's the first thing anyone has said on the walk here. Because what is there to say? If Nick's right, Mr. Lewis is dying. And they are going to visit him.

Cassie's scared.

She thinks everyone is scared. Not because they skipped out of school. Though she's pretty sure no one in this group has done that before. Not even because skipping is going to make those meetings with Mr. Deming worse. Just because . . . what will they say to Mr. Lewis?

They all hesitate a second before they turn up the drive, their feet stuttering on the sidewalk. They cluster behind Nick as he reaches out, knocks on the cheerful door.

It's weird to be following Nick. He didn't used to be someone people followed. But right now, he's clearly the leader. Following seems right.

It's a while before someone opens the door. Cassie has time to notice a tiny nest with a yellow bird in it buried in the bush. She sees that three rusty bolts have left streaks on the downspout. She sees that Mac nicked himself twice when he cleaned up his shave. She feels the odd, new sensation of the breeze blowing across her bald head.

The door opens. A woman with gray hair looks out at them

through the screen door with a guarded expression.

"Mrs. Lewis?" Nick starts. Then he doesn't seem to know where to go from there.

The woman swings the screen door open and stares. "Nicholas Finlay? Is that you?" Her face cycles through surprise, then tenderness, then something that looks a lot like amusement, before it drops back into a tired sadness. "Oh dear," she says. "Just a minute. He really didn't want anyone to know. He was trying to avoid . . . oh dear. Wait right here, okay?"

This time it takes forever before she comes back. Mac is cracking his knuckles repeatedly, which is driving Cassie crazy. Jake's bouncing up and down on his heels on a squeaky porch board, which may be driving her crazier. She's counting every rivet in the gutters. Wondering where that fleece beanie she had last winter is. Also, considering slugging Mac and Jake. *Aaaaah, hold* still, *you guys.*

Finally, there are steps coming toward them in the house. The door sweeps open again. Mrs. Lewis is saying, "Come in, come in. Sorry to keep you waiting." They follow her down a hall with bright paintings framed on the walls.

She pauses outside a door. Gives Nick a sharp look. "Short visit, Nicholas. He needs to rest." Nick nods. And they go in.

Mr. Lewis is propped up in one of those beds they have in hospitals with the railings on the sides. He looks like regular Mr. Lewis—flyaway hair, crooked smile—except he's in pajamas, and he has two clear plastic tubes running up into his nose.

They all kind of do their nervous pause thing again. But then Nick walks across the floor, sits down in the chair next to the bed, and reaches out and puts his hand over Mr. Lewis's hand lying on the blanket. So they follow Nick. End up in an awkward clump by the side of the bed.

Mr. Lewis looks them over. Flashes them a big, lopsided grin. The kind of grin he gives them when he's hugely amused by something. Like when Jake thinks no one knows he's watching Lily while she plays, and he forgets to come in at the right time, and Mr. Lewis grins and says, "Mr. Cranch, coming in three measures late is not improvisation. It's just not paying attention. Let's try that again." But this time, the grin turns into a funny little wheezy laugh.

Cassie doesn't know what he's laughing at. But after a while his laugh makes her smile. A chuckle breaks out from Mac. Jake giggles. Then Cassie and Nick glance at each other and crack up. And whatever it is seems funnier and funnier until they're all a ridiculous laughing mess. Everyone in the room laughing along with Mr. Lewis at whatever Mr. Lewis is laughing at. Mac is straight-up snort-giggling.

And then Mr. Lewis starts coughing. And coughing.

And nothing's funny anymore. They look at each other, panicked, but Nick reaches over and helps Mr. Lewis sit up a little higher on the pillows, and the coughing finally stops. Mr.

Lewis wipes his eyes and smiles at them again. He gestures, grinning, at their bald heads. "Ummm, kids, I appreciate the show of support, but I'm not doing chemo this time."

So Nick's right. Mr. Lewis is really, really sick. So sick that he won't be getting better.

NICK

What They Tell Him

THEY DON'T STAY LONG. Nick knows Mrs. Lewis was serious about that.

But they stay long enough to tell him the story of the performance last night and how they thought he'd left because of the budget cuts and why they shaved their heads. How they had this whole light show and pictures flashing on the walls and a protest banner and how the audience went straight-up crazy.

They tell him how they played, how everybody listened to everybody else, how they riffed off each other, how the music was beyond awesome. And he says he wishes he'd been there to see it; it sounds like it was something else. They tell him someone put part of it up on the internet, and he grins and says, "Send me the link."

Then he lays his head back on his pillow and looks at them, still smiling, but Nick can see he's tired.

Anyway, Mrs. Lewis comes in and says, "All right, you guys. Enough for now." And even though Mr. Lewis kind of waves her off, Nick knows they have to go. But, because he also knows that sometimes you don't get another chance to say what you came to say, Nick tells him, "Thanks for teaching us to play," and everybody is nodding and saying, "Yeah, thanks. Thanks."

And they know it's not enough. But Mr. Lewis knows what they mean. He knows.

JAKE

Talking to Lily

WHEN THEY GET OUT on the sidewalk, everybody is kind of quiet, and Mac is wiping his eyes on his sleeve, and Jake's not quite sure what to do. "Hey, why isn't Lily at school today?" he asks Cassie. She gets those two little lines over her nose that mean she's worried.

"Lily's in big trouble," Cassie says. "Her dad's way super mad about the hair. And about us getting called in by Deming. Her dad says we're a bad influence. He's pulling her out of Jazz Lab and making her go back to orchestra."

"What?" says Nick.

And Mac is like, "No way. No way."

"It's true," Cassie says. "They had a humongous fight." Everyone turns and starts back up the street toward the school, talking about it. But Jake's still standing at Mr. Lewis's gate.

Mac turns around. "Jake, you coming?"

"Go on ahead," Jake tells them. "I'll be back a little later."

Because he's not coming.

He's going to talk to Lily.

Jake's walking through the streets of town in the opposite direction from school, probably on his way to his own death, because Mr. Messina is one of those dads who bury the bones of guys who come to talk to their daughters in the backyard, but Jake doesn't even care because Lily can't, can't, can't leave Jazz Lab or the whole world will be ruined.

The town is being invaded by dying mayflies today—little whiskery-tailed corpses lying on the shelf below the ATM at KeyBank and drifting into the cracks of the sidewalk. Jake goes down Laurel and past the shops on Lake Street, past the Episcopal church with the big red doors, and turns into that lane that, since fifth grade, he's known leads to Lily's house but he has never, ever walked down.

This time, he walks down it. Repeating under his breath what he wants to say. Down to the big white house on the big green lawn by the big blue lake and up the wide, stone steps, crunching through crowds of rigor mortis mayflies and trying not to pay attention to the fact that his heart is beating faster than a Max Roach drum solo. He's pretty sure that is not healthy. It will be completely awkward if he dies on Lily Messina's classy blue-and-white WE WELCOME YOU TO OUR HOME doormat.

Now his knees have gotten into the act, and they're knocking out a nice rhythmic "Gonna die, gonna die, gonna die, die,

die," but his hand reaches up and rings the doorbell anyway. He's praying that Lily herself will answer the door, or Lily's sister or her mom or her second cousin's uncle from Cleveland, and Jake doesn't know what's going on with his prayers lately, but there seems to be a big problem in the translation department, because the door swings open, and there's Mr. Messina.

Who really is a substantial man when you get up close. He's filling up this whole entryway with his big shoulders and his big jaw and his big pale-blue dress shirt. Who wears a dress shirt at home? Also, his mustache looks dangerous. And his hands. Giant hands with huge knuckles and a couple of muscular gold rings on big fingers. He will reach out with those enormous hands, and Jake will feel them go around his throat and tighten, and the posts of the porch will go all gray and fuzzy in front of his eyes. All he can hope for is that he blacks out before his neck snaps.

Mr. Messina clears his throat. He's looking at Jake in a way that clearly says, "There is an idiot standing on my porch, and he has exactly two-point-three seconds to make his intentions known, or I will drop-kick him out into my elegant shrubberies." But it's awfully hard to respond in a timely manner when Jake's busy uncollapsing his throat and trying to keep his knees from shattering each other, and when his out-of-control circulatory system is about to explode all over the Messinas' porch.

"You can't make Lily leave Jazz Lab," says Jake. "Because she is a really good bass player. Really good. And she should get to play." And he wishes his voice hadn't gone quite so high at the end and that he could get his knees under control, but there, he said it.

"Excuse me?" says Mr. Messina, and Jake wonders how much longer this circulatory madness can go on before he just expires on the porch. So it's a good thing that, at this moment, Lily comes clattering down the stairs.

She freezes when she sees him standing outside the door. Now that her hair is gone, it's like her brown eyes are enormous in her face. Like Jake can't not look at her eyes. Even though her dad is looking at him looking.

Which he is. "Five minutes," he says to Jake. "Stay where I can see you."

Jeez. What does he think Jake came to do?

Lily's blushing, but she motions Jake back through a big, superclean kitchen and opens a glass door, and they walk together across the lawn, a new hatch of little mayflies letting go of the blades of grass as they pass so that it looks like they're walking through a snowstorm, except the flakes fall upward—up and up into the blue spring sky until they disappear into the sun.

Lily sits down on a wall near the edge of the lake. Jake sits next to her. They both look out over the water where the sun glints and dances. Delicate patterns of light and shadow shimmer over the rocks just below their feet. Jake is sitting on a warm stone wall by a deep blue lake and he's sitting next to Lily Messina. The world has never been so beautiful.

"You can't quit," Jake says. "No matter what your dad says. You can't quit Jazz Lab."

LILY

Something to Say

"DAD?" LILY KNOCKS ON THE DOORJAMB of her dad's office, even though the door is half-open. Her dad's not at his desk. He's standing by one of the windows, staring out at the lake.

Lily wonders if he was there the whole time Jake and she were talking.

Doesn't matter. She was surprised to see Jake on her doorstep, but she's glad he came. She's glad it matters to him that she stays in Jazz Lab. She's glad he understands how she feels about playing the bass. She's glad he was the one to tell her about Mr. Lewis being sick.

"Dad?" she says again. "I have something to say, and I need you to listen to me, okay?"

He turns partway toward her. His face is still in the shadow thrown by the drapes, but the sun coming through the windowpane lays down a lattice across his blue shirt.

"I want to stay in Jazz Lab," says Lily. "And in Jazz Ensemble next year, even if Mr. Lewis isn't the one teaching it. Because I am good at bass like Jake said, but also because even if I wasn't good at it, playing jazz makes me happy, and being with my friends makes me happy."

"I wish you hadn't cut off your hair," her dad says. "What did the hair have to do with it?"

"Were you listening to me before the hair?"

Her dad turns the rest of the way toward her, so his face is in the light from the window. He looks tired. Or sad maybe.

"Jake and I are going to walk up to the school now, okay?" says Lily. "We want to get there while the other kids from Jazz Lab are still at lunch."

"Are you asking me or telling me?"

"Both," says Lily.

QUAGMIRE

All In

IT'S TEN MINUTES BEFORE THE END of English when the announcement system clicks on and Deming's voice pours into the room: "The following students please report immediately to the main office," he says. Quag wonders idly about the word "main." It's not like there's a whole string of offices. Only one. So what's with the "main"? The voice continues: "Cassandra Byzinski, Jacob Cranch, Nicholas Finlay, Lily Messina, McKay Silva."

Perfect. Couldn't be better. Trust Deming to be prompt with the smackdown. Apparently, Mr. Saavedra didn't rat Quag out to Deming about the sound booth stuff since his name isn't on the list. But this doesn't look good for the Jazz Lab kids.

Lily is slowly putting her books in her backpack. Jake is trying to stuff all his papers back in his folder, and Quag can see that Jake's hands are shaking. Kids like Jake and Lily aren't used to being in trouble. Deming will eat them alive.

Quag gets to his feet.

Harken gives him a stern look from over her glasses. "Sit down, please, Mr. Tiarello," she says.

"I'm going with them," says Quag.

"Of course you are," Harken says. "When they go." Harken turns toward Lily. "Ms. Messina, Mr. Cranch, if you could please sit back down also." Jake sinks slowly into his seat. Lily stops trying to zip her backpack.

Ms. Harken sighs. "There are only ten minutes left in this class. We are just beginning the first chapter of Kekla Magoon's fine book, and you will not understand a thing that happens without that first chapter, so I think ten minutes from now is immediate enough for all of us, don't you?"

Sam Armitage unfolds his big self from his chair. "I'm going with them too," he says.

Now Gina Yoon is out of her seat, followed quickly by Dante Lake. "Me too," they say in unison. Then Archie Block is up. Archie, who with his newly shaved head has the most perfectly round face of anyone Quag has ever seen. Aisha Rodriguez is standing by her chair. Chieko Wright. Oren Powless. Terrell and Christa Freeman, both bald and looking very much like the twins they are without the different hairdos. More and more people around the room stand. A lot of kids are still sitting, looking nervously around, but at least half the students are on their feet.

Ms. Harken slides a bookmark into her book and closes it. She scans the room. "I understand why Mr. Tiarello would feel that he needs to accompany Lily and Jake to the office. However, I'm curious about the reasoning from the rest of you."

"Because they were trying to help us keep wood shop here and all the rest. So they shouldn't be the only ones to get in trouble when they wanted to help everyone," says Sam.

"Is that accurate?" Harken asks the rest of the students standing.

There are nods from around the room.

"Ah," says Ms. Harken. She folds her hands over her book. "In that case, perhaps the first chapter can wait until Monday. Quagmire, can you please lead the students who are already standing down to the office?"

So that's what Quag did.

QUAGMIRE

A Question

QUAG STICKS HIS HEAD through the door of Ms. Harken's room. She's sitting at her desk, working her way briskly through a stack of papers. When she notices Quag, she raises her eyebrows like she's asking a question without asking a question.

"He gave everyone detention," says Quag. "All of us."

"You don't sound surprised," says Ms. Harken.

Quag shrugs. It's not like Deming is exactly the king of creativity. With him, it's either a lecture or detention, or suspension if he can get away with it. The guy didn't even come out of his office to talk to them. Saw them coming, closed the door, and called out on his phone to tell the receptionists to give them all detention slips. And when they didn't leave, he called out again to say that for every thirty minutes they were not in their regularly assigned classes, he would add another day of detention.

He may have called out a third time, Quag thinks he did, but that time Jake's mom didn't pick up—she and the other receptionist shared a glance, and both let the phone ring. So far, Quag figures everybody's up to four days of detention, and nobody's left the office yet. The kids are actually kind of excited, like they think they're really doing something.

But Quag's not seeing it. How's this going to get them anything? So when no one was paying attention, he came down to talk to Harken for a minute. Which seems like maybe a dumb idea now.

Ms. Harken laces her fingers together and rests her chin on her fists. "Mr. Tiarello, what is a hierarchical system?"

Yeah, definitely a dumb idea.

Quag shoots Harken a look. He is not planning on suddenly becoming the kind of kid who answers questions just because someone feels like asking them. He's not even sure why he came here.

Ms. Harken pushes back from her desk. She uncaps a marker and starts drawing a diagram on the whiteboard. "A hierarchy is interested in who has formal authority over whom. So a teacher might have formal authority over a student, and a principal might have formal authority over a teacher." She draws a circle above the principal. "Normally, the superintendent has formal authority over a principal, but at the moment we only have an interim superintendent who is just biding his time till a new one can be hired and won't get involved." She caps her marker and chooses another. "But a school is complex, so it's never quite that simple, is it? There are other groups that have power—the teachers' union, the school board, parents."

Ms. Harken turns toward Quag. "And there are other types of power than formal authority. In fact, I think you, especially, know something about wielding informal power, Mr. Tiarello. And it is good for certain things, as you and your friends demonstrated last night. However, you may be overlooking a few possibilities that could bolster your efforts in a more formal way."

Quag stares at Harken. *Get on with it.*

Harken draws a circle around the word "parents" and around "school board." "We have an election coming up in two weeks. Students will not be allowed to vote, but parents will. And not all the candidates agree with the current board's philosophy. In fact, there are quite a few running this time who do not."

"Which ones?" Quag asks. He realizes this is the first question he has asked a teacher in years, and he gives Harken a scowl just in case she's going to make a big deal out of it, but she isn't paying attention. She digs through the top drawer in her desk, then steps toward him holding out a flyer with the words "Southton Falls School Board Candidates" on it.

Now Ms. Harken is examining Quagmire over the top of those glasses of hers. Her eyes are a deep brown. "Anyone who is intelligent enough to take over a concert in the way you did last night is certainly intelligent enough to figure out the answer to that question himself," she says. She holds out the flyer again.

Quag hesitates.

"Cassie and Gina and Dante may be interested in this also," says Harken.

So Quag takes it. For Cassie.

NICK

In the Loop

NICK STOPS BY LEWIS'S on the way home a few days after their first visit. Mrs. Lewis opens the door, and she looks way tired. "Not today, Nicholas. He's sleeping today," she says. Her face makes him remember how tired he felt that last week with his grandad. How he didn't want to go to sleep at all, even though Grandad was mostly asleep all the time. Nick was scared Grandad might die while Nick was asleep. Like somehow Nick being awake was keeping him here.

Stupid, he knows. But still. It felt that way.

"Mrs. Lewis?" She's turning to go, and Nick doesn't want to be a jerk, but he needs to ask her one thing. "Will you text us when . . . ?" And then he feels his face flame hot because, never mind, he is a total, complete jerk, because he can see from her face that they both know that he just pretty much said, "Hey, let me know when your husband dies." He can't breathe right for a minute. His ears are so hot he feels like they might catch on fire.

"It's okay, Nick," she says.

So then he makes it worse by blurting out, "But you will, right?"

"Honey, I'll talk to your mom about this. I'll keep you in the loop, okay?"

"Okay," Nick says. "Okay." And he takes off down the steps.

When he turns at the gate to wave, she's already back inside, door closed.

So that weekend, when the phone rings during dinner, and Nick's mom answers it, puts her hand over her heart, and then leans her forehead against the faded blue chicken wallpaper in the kitchen, he knows exactly what's happened even before she says it.

He gets out his phone and, hands shaking, opens the Jazz Lab group chat and tells everyone that Mr. Lewis has died. And then, because he does feel, after everything they've done together, that he really is part of the group, he asks for something. He asks if they can meet at Lakeside Park to talk. And they all say yes.

LILY

Crying in the Kitchen

LILY DOESN'T KNOW what her face looks like when she comes into the kitchen, but her mom just stands up from the table where she's working on her computer and holds her arms out to Lily like she used to when Lily was little and had fallen down and scraped up her knees. And Lily goes to her exactly like that too and buries her face in her mom's shirt and cries while her mom says, "It's all right, baby. It'll be all right." After a while, Lily finally sobs out what's happened, and her mom hugs her tighter and tells her how sorry she is. Lily can feel her mom's tears falling onto her scalp as she holds her. And by then, Nonna has made her way into the kitchen and put another layer on the whole big teary hug.

"My friends are all going to the park to talk," Lily tells her mom. "I want to go."

She hears the jangle of someone taking keys down from the hook by the bulletin board, and her dad says, "I'll drive you."

"That's all right, Marius. I can take her," says her mom,

and Lily can hear by the crispness in her voice that she's still way mad at Dad about how he's behaved toward Lily since the concert. Part of Lily wants to be mad too and turn her back on him and walk out and let him see what that feels like. But another part of her knows there's such a bigger thing going on right now that she doesn't even care about that. So she says, "It's okay, Mom. Dad can drive me."

"Well, he might want to only drive, then, and not talk too much," Nonna pipes up. "Since there have been some not-so-smart things coming out of his mouth lately."

And he doesn't talk too much. He opens the car door for Lily and drives to the park and says, "Take as long as you need, honey," when she gets out of the car. "I know this is important."

"I'll text you," she says.

And then Cassie is running across the grass toward her, and Cassie is crying in a harsh, tearing way like things are coming apart inside her, and it's Lily's turn to open her arms and say, "It's all right, Cassie. It'll be all right."

JAKE

Playing Through

JAKE DOESN'T KNOW what to think. His chest feels tight, like someone is standing on it, and he wants to go to the park and talk, but he is scared to go. Still, he goes out the door and down Laurel and across the street near Ten Spot Gifts and over to Lakeside Park. When he gets there and sees Cassie standing in the shadow of the gazebo, sobbing like her heart is floating around in her chest in a thousand sharp-edged pieces that are hurting her every time she breathes in, he sure wishes he hadn't come.

But he makes his feet go across the grass toward her. And then Lily gets out of a car, and Cassie runs to her, and Nick shows up with some of those candles like you light in church, and Mac comes carrying two bags of Milky Ways like that's something you'd bring to a thing like this, and Jake's chest loosens, and he thinks, *It's gonna be okay. Because we're all here and we'll play through, and we'll find what comes next. Just like Mr. Lewis taught us.*

QUAGMIRE

Replay

QUAG PULLS UP THE VIDEO on his phone and watches it again as he lies in bed. It's a crap recording done by some kid who was sitting in the audience with his phone, but even so, you can see how amazing it was. Especially the images Quag threw across the walls of the auditorium. Man, he's proud of those. Even though it took him all night and some climbing up in the catwalks above the auditorium—which would probably have been frowned on by the powers that be—to figure out how to get them up there. It was worth it.

He watches the images flashing on the screen as the video pans across the room—photos of people carrying protest signs, and then pictures of kids in the middle school, and photos of other protest signs he and Cassie painted up in the sound booth during a lull in drama rehearsals while the cast ran that doomed dance number in the second act over and over and over down onstage. STOP STARVING OUR FUTURE. ARTS MATTER. INVEST IN US. WE WANT A VOICE IN WHAT WE LEARN. LISTEN UP! He remembers how she kept tucking her hair behind her ear and it kept falling out, the smudge of red paint across the back of her hand, how her orange fingernail polish was chipped and a little ragged. How intense she always was. Like whatever she was doing right then was the most important thing anyone had ever done.

He lets himself wish for just a second that Saavedra hadn't kicked him off crew.

Whatever.

Still worth it.

Cassie and Gina and Dante called a bunch of the school board candidates. And then Quag and Jake went with them when they visited this guy named Khalil Taylor, who was up on a ladder getting his kids' Frisbee off the roof but came down and talked to them for a while. Turned out Khalil had been in Harken's class when he was in middle school. "Yeah," he said. "Harken's got a soft spot for nonconformists," and he laughed. He introduced them to a couple of his friends who are also running for the school board and who seem more okay than most adults.

And Jake lost it and attacked the campaign sign for his aunt in his front yard with his clarinet case until it was a crumpled mess, so that was worth seeing. Then Jake put up four yard signs for other candidates, so no doubt there would be interesting drama over that move to hear about at the lunch table.

And that concert. That concert.

So, yeah. Definitely worth it.

CASSIE

Coming into Focus

AUNT BECCA LETS CASSIE USE her darkroom when she's home. Most of Becca's stuff is shot digitally, but Aunt Bec still loves film. She says film is half history, half magic. She shoots a lot of the projects she does for fun on film.

Cassie likes being in the darkroom. She likes when her eyes get used to the dimness and she's standing there in the glow of the orange lights, watching the image slowly appear.

It does seem like magic then. Like somehow she had nothing to do with putting that picture on the paper, and she holds her breath and waits to see what appears. A face. A leaf curled in the wind. A hand reaching out for hers.

The morning after Mr. Lewis dies, Cassie gets out her phone and sets it on the bedspread in front of her. She thinks about Mr. Lewis. Closes her eyes and lets herself see his smile, his funny, floaty hair, his hands. She remembers the concert. Lets herself see each of her friends' faces as they played together. Lets herself feel Quag's fingers on her jaw again. She thinks about what it feels like to be part of something that's not just you. She looks at the moving boxes still stacked on her floor.

Aunt Becca is on a project that she spent two years lining up grants for. But Cassie lets herself see a picture, lets the image come clear. How it could look to stay here, to stay with people she loves and who love her enough to shape their lives around hers. She finally finds the words to text Aunt Becca what she's been wanting to say for weeks: "Can you please come home right now? I need you."

She hits SEND.

LILY

Together

IT'S BEEN MORE THAN A WEEK since Mr. Lewis died. They've been through the funeral, all of Jazz Lab sitting together. They've been through the strange couple of days after the funeral where everything seemed so final, and all Lily wanted to do was sit on the couch with Nonna, leaning against her, feeling Nonna hold her hand.

Then, on the Monday morning after the funeral, Mac texts, "Bring instruments, meet at front steps now." Lily knows her dad might actually let her go, but it would definitely mean a whole long discussion about it first. She's glad they're talking more, but they're still awkward at it, and she doesn't want to deal with that right now, so she just grabs her bass and heads out the door without talking to anyone. She doesn't even stop to put it in its case.

It's kind of hard sneaking out of the house with a bass. Makes her wish she played the flute or something. But she gets her arms around it and lugs it down the long driveway, hoping no one looks out the window.

By the time she reaches the end of the driveway, she's sweating and wondering how she's going to drag it all the way to school without her arms falling off. But then she hears the whir of wheels, and when she looks up, it's Jake riding toward her on a skateboard. He waves and hops off, and they put the skateboard under the bass and, walking on either side, steer it toward school together.

It's one of those days when upstate New York is making up for the whole gray winter and uneasy spring by letting you know that spring is here to stay, and there are birds singing and sticky leaves uncurling and a breeze brushing the back of your neck. It feels like the whole world is trying to help you be a little happier after a hard time.

When they get to the school, Mac's wrestling a keyboard and amp out of his family's van, and Cassie has a big black-and-white photo of Mr. Lewis that she's putting on Nick's music stand like an easel while Nick writes *Rest In Peace, Mr. Lewis* on the sidewalk with chalk. Jake gets his clarinet out of his backpack and comes over to stand next to Lily.

And everyone just knows what to do. They let Mac start them off with some sweet, sad melody that makes your throat hurt, and they all follow him. They play as the sun reaches out across the grass. They play as the teachers start to come in. Some of the teachers stop and stand with their heads bowed for a few minutes. Some smile sadly at them. Mr. Saavedra gives a little fist thump to his heart as he passes. And Mr. Conroy stands for a long time and cries, tears running down his face into his beard. He took band with Mr. Lewis back when he was in high school. Lily remembers Mr. Conroy talking about that once.

Then the kids come off the buses and out of their parents' cars or walk down the street. Some stop and listen. Quag gives them a nod as he passes, and Cassie nods back as she plays. Some of the kids write messages on the sidewalk with the chalk. Some have tears in their eyes, and Lily doesn't know whether the tears are for Mr. Lewis or for what they all tried to do together at the concert and what that felt like. Maybe both.

They've still got the meetings with Deming to face. They don't know if Cassie's dad will let her stay with Aunt Becca. They don't know who will win the school board election, though they're working hard on that. They aren't sure if they've saved anything at all. And even if they've saved some things, Jazz Lab and Jazz Ensemble won't be what they were without Mr. Lewis.

But their parents are listening now. Or a lot of them are. Their parents are talking with them and with other parents about what they can do. And kids from all over the school are talking to other kids they never used to talk to. So they have that.

And they have each other. They play through the warning bell. They play through the tardy bell. They play through everyone going into the school to start the day. When they finally stop, Nick steps out from the group and plays taps all alone. After that, everyone's a little teary, but it doesn't matter. They pack up their instruments and sit down on the grass and laugh a little about how they're all crying a little. And then they sit together and remember. "Remember when Mr. Lewis laughed so hard that he spit Diet Coke all over his shirt?" "Remember how his hair kind of floated?" "Remember when he made Nick play his shoe?" And that feels good.

Here is what Lily knows. She knows that the sun is warm and the sky is blue and that she and Cassie will always be friends. No matter where Cassie ends up living. She knows that they were lucky to have a teacher like Mr. Lewis. She knows that she wants to be with her friends in Jazz Lab this year and Jazz Ensemble next year, whatever those look like, whatever they can make them. She knows you have to listen to each other while you play if you want to make something beautiful.

They didn't know their lives would change this year. It seemed like a regular year. Regular stuff. Regular problems. But then it wasn't. They did something big when they spoke up at the concert. Even though they were kind of wrong about what was going on with Mr. Lewis, what they all did together was important. Is still important.

Lily leans back and listens to Nick talking to Cassie about the guy who invented the saxophone. She hears Mac tapping out a rhythm on the side of the amp while he tells Jake a joke. Jake is smiling at her while he listens to Mac. Lily smiles back. A little breeze drifts around them, carrying the scent of something leafy and the clear smell of the lake.

Today feels sad, sweet, strong—everything. Like they've played through the turnaround, and they're headed into the next part of the tune. Together.

ACKNOWLEDGMENTS

Perhaps there are writers who travel swiftly and elegantly through the wilderness called Novel, but I am not one of those. So to everyone who helped push, pull, coax, and carry me across, heartfelt thanks.

Special thanks to:

All the kids who have hung out at my house over the years in Michigan, Minnesota, and New York. Thank you for adding so much fun to my life and to my children's lives, and for reminding me how much you have to offer the world if the adults can only get their act together and listen to you.

Patti Gauch, for putting so many tools in my writer's toolbox and for always making the journey an adventure.

Erin Murphy, for showing me what it means to be a mensch in a tough business and for waiting patiently while I figured out how to write a novel.

Anne Hoppe, for having a bigger vision for this book, helping me see that vision, and then lending me her brilliant mind to help me make it happen. I have never been in better hands. It's been a joy to work with her.

Eleanor Hinkle, for being this story's first champion at

Clarion, for great feedback about some of the things that just weren't working yet, and for your helpfulness throughout the process.

Anna Dobbin, for saving me from my tenuous grip on timelines, among other things, and for being just so dang elegant in how she fixed some of my awkward sentences that it made my writerly heart sing. Anything that is still wonky in this novel is because I didn't fix it, not because Anna didn't catch it, I promise you.

Artist Chris Danger, for his brilliant composition, dazzling artwork, and thoughtful commitment to getting everything just right. It was such a joy to get a look at the cover and feel this sense of recognition: "Those are my kids!" Designer Natalie Sousa, for knowing Chris was the right artist for the book, her inspired design, tireless attention to detail, and love of saxophones. And art director Samira Iravani, for knowing Natalie was the right designer for the book and bringing her own sharp insight to the project. In spite of the adage, everyone judges a book by its cover, so thanks to the team for creating a cover that so brilliantly telegraphs what's in the pages inside. I'm deeply grateful.

Sondra Soderborg, for being my writing buddy for more years than either of us probably wants to count and for putting up with me even back in the days when it was the blind leading the blind and we both regularly ended up in the ditch. ("I have an idea. White space!") It makes me beyond happy that our first novels are coming out in the same year.

Christine Carron, Charlie Perryess, Lisze Bechtold, Louisa Jaggar, Sharon Dembro, Sondra Soderborg, Stella Michel, Susan Wheeler, and Tara Carson, for being just the sorts of generous souls I want to travel with. Thank you for the discussions about structure, the beta reads, the jazz CDs sent from New Orleans, the encouragement, the smart critiques. And thank you for never saying out loud, "Good grief, Larsen. Are you *still* working on that?"

Kate and Tim, for living with the Jazz Lab kids so long that they almost seem like siblings and for being my most honest readers. Thanks to Kate for rioting semiweekly until there was more of Mac, and to Tim for letting me steal his good lines.

And finally, Dave Larsen, for always giving me the space and support I need to be creative and for being at least 2.73 times as excited about every good thing that happens as I am. We have a book, kid! I couldn't have done it without you.

ABOUT THE AUTHOR

Unlike the kids in Jazz Lab, Mylisa Larsen does not play any instruments well, (though there is a long-suffering piano in her life). But she loves listening to people who do. So she was pretty happy that writing this book gave her the excuse to listen to a whole lot of jazz, both old and new.

Mylisa was born in Idaho but has since lived in eight states and two countries, and she has loved things about all of them. She now lives in upstate New York with her family and a sweet but somewhat neurotic dog who is convinced that pirates are trying to break into the house at all hours. She is the author of several picture books. *Playing Through the Turnaround* is her first novel.

You can visit her on the web at mylisalarsen.com.